Published by CLASH Books, Troy, NY.

clashbooks.com

CLASH

FICTION

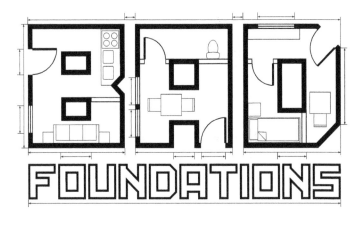

AUTHOR: **Brian Allen Carr**	PUBLISHER: CLASH Books
TITLE: Bad Foundations	

TABLE OF CONTENTS 5

For Taylor Swift

My kids will probably spend my royalties
on your merch, so I might as well
dedicate the whole book to you.

QUICK LOOKING OUT:

I spend a lot of time talking to an imaginary version of Mary Louise Kelly—out loud and to myself.

The real Mary Louise Kelly interviews people for NPR.

I was supposed to meet her, and she was supposed to interview me with a few other writers, but we had a pandemic instead.

The universe is a process, I'm told.

I spend a lot of time driving—a lot of time alone—and my mind runs and runs and I'll answer pretend questions as I drive my Prius down the highway.

"Funny you should ask, Imagination Mary Louise Kelly," I say whenever I feel like a question has been asked—whenever I have some big idea I want to say. "Maybe it's about perspective. Maybe we've moved beyond the absurd. We're stuck in an endless process we can't fathom. Up until now, we've seen it all wrong—lived a reversed myth. In reality, the rock smiles, let's go of Sisyphus, and rolls back down the hill."

This is one of the ways I sprang from the unfathomable process of the universe: my great-grandfather was a ditch digger in Texas. He did Public Works projects on the Houston Ship Channel. He had uncomfortable false teeth that he kept in his back pocket for when around people and every time he accidentally sat on them, he said, "Oops, I bit my own ass."

My grandfather, his son, sold insurance.

When he was fifteen, he lied about his age and enlisted as a Marine to fight in WWII.

He deployed to the Eastern Front. He was shot in the head, nearly lost both feet to frostbite, and was pitched into a tree by a grenade. The grenade killed his best friend, and my grandfather lived the rest of his life with shrapnel in his leg and would wake screaming in his twisted-up sheets when his blackened feet ached with phantom frostbite—his doctors wanted to amputate, he somehow shewed them away. When the war ended, he was 17.

He used to always say, "Life is what you make it." When he farted, he'd say, "Catch that and paint it green." If asked by his children, "What's for dinner?" he said, "Dead dog, stewed cat, dish rot, mutton."

I never met him. Never heard any of this firsthand. He drank a lot of scotch, smoked Marlboros all day, wasn't happy unless he was hunting or fishing, and dropped dead at 48.

His oldest child, my mother, is a nurse. She's been at the same hospital for twenty years and has worked her way into hospital administration. She wants to die drinking margaritas on a sailboat.

Me, I get bored easily.

I could change jobs every year.

I have taught college. I have sold cars.

For the most part, I preferred car sales, but somehow, when I taught college, it felt like my great-grandfather was back in history with a nice job and pretty teeth—smiling.

I guess I understand the motions.

We see what we want to see.

"Exactly," I say to Imagination Mary Louise Kelly, picking up our endless conversation—if it's ever been left off. "In that case, you'd be right. The world would be a strange one. Inside out. Upside down. Backwards from conception. And every time a person fails, a rock rolls down toward heaven."

1

They live in old Victorians with red brick foundations—cellars of stagnant air, perfumed by decades of dust. In side-gabled Tudors with concrete-wrapped porches that sink from the home's fascia—cracks in the stoop. In Craftsmen, in Queen Annes, in mid-century moderns. In stone-façade, single-level ranches—mortar crumbling from joints. Split-level contemporaries with differential settlement. Asymmetrical Mansards with penicillium on the joists. Modern internationals, "The windows won't open." Deeply ornamented Chateauesques, "See, all the doors stick."

They're renting. They're buying. They inherited it outright. They've lived there forever. They sell in three days. "Depending on what you tell me," they tell me. "Depending on what you say."

I mainly work in crawl spaces. I inspect bad foundations.

Pretend you're my customer.

You have called me out to your house because you have cracks in your walls, or sloping floors that bounce and wobble, or the whole home smells like it was milked from a sock.

"Why are these here?" You ask, pointing at the cracks in your walls. You had never once thought about your house as a thing that might fall apart beneath you. You are shocked that it is something that anyone could endure. "It's a well-made house," you tell me. "But this cabinet shakes every time I do this." You sort of bounce on the floor in front of the cabinet and your gewgaws and bric-à-brac shimmy on the shelves. "But it's a good home. Sturdy. Except for this." You bounce and jostle it all again.

In some unfortunate instances, homes were even built by a family member, inherited after the builder's traumatic death. The Uncle who could fix everything, claimed by cancer, claimed by age. Slunk back into the recesses of the home to sleep forever in memory.

"It could be a few different things," I'll tell you. "Differential settlement. Rot. Compression. It's either too much weight or too much water. Time and gravity take their toll. Entropy, I guess. It all moves toward disorder."

"I think it's just what happens," you might venture. "Over the years. Things crack."

Some customers have me out to defend their home's integrity. It isn't a trial. There are no jurors. There is evidence, and there are tools. Your senses tell you the symptoms; the tools tell you the cause. After that, there's no debate: the tools don't lie. Not understanding this, or being mired in denial, some customers slip into jargon and posit theories.

"This home was built in 1957," they argue. "Sixty-five years ago. Isn't that old for a house?"

"Sort of."

"And I don't even understand the point of crawl spaces."

"It's. . ."

"Shouldn't they build them different?"

"How?"

"I don't know. My next house is gonna have a basement."

"They can be worse."

"What about concrete ones?"

"Slabs."

"Slabs?"

"Concrete slab foundations."

"Yes. Slabs. I'll get a slab."

"They can be just as problematic. Even more expensive to fix if things go wrong."

"More expensive?"

"More expensive."

"Then what do you do? What doesn't break?"

"It all breaks. Everything. Eventually."

Many customers haven't done research, so I teach them. Sometimes they get confused. Sometimes they've lived their whole lives in their house and didn't know they had a crawl space at all.

"Underneath me?" they say when I show them inspection pictures. "That's been under me this whole time?"

A universe of filth, right beneath their feet. The exact footprint of their house with three-foot high joist-exposed ceilings and a mud and gravel floor. Unexplored. Unkempt. Unremembered. Cobwebbed.

Here's how I learned about crawl spaces:

I was fifteen years old, and I met a boy whose father died in a crawl space. So, I looked up "crawl space" in my World Book Encyclopedia, and I thought, "how bad would life have to be to work in there, and how lonely to die that way?"

My encyclopedia had gold-dipped page edges. The crawl space pictures were diagrams in black ink. But still, I could tell they were terrible places. Confined. Stagnant. Packed with critters and bugs.

There was a write-up about his death in the paper. The house where he died was a few blocks from mine. I walked by it 1,000 times trying to coax myself to look inside. The paper didn't say exactly what killed him. I made it as far as the crawl space door with a flashlight in my hand but couldn't make myself open it.

The customers who learn about their crawl spaces from me have no sense of what home repair costs.

"It's not expensive," they'll say. "Is it?" Their eyes show fear, anguish, anger, dismay. "To fix something like this?" They'll point at the cracks. "Does it have to mean something?"

I'll wait several beats. I'll breathe deep and contemplate what they are contemplating, willing all the silence to become heavy, and waiting a bit longer until the silence doubles in weight. Doubles in weight again. Sits upon us like stench. The light of the home pulses. The mechanicals—air conditioning, water heater, refrigerator—hum. "Unfortunately," I'll tell them, "Every crack is a cause for concern."

THINGS RECENTLY BLAMED ON JP

Ticket on 465, pulled over for going too slow. The speed limit was 55 and I was going 55. The cop told me, "You have to keep up with traffic." And I said, "What if traffic is going 100 miles an hour?" Technically my ticket was for not being able to find my proof of insurance. I could have found it. I needed more time. I got pulled over for going "slow." "Slow" was the speed limit.

Lost laser tape in crawl in Terre Haute. The furthest town I go to stole one of my favorite tools.

Opened a crawl door in Mooresville and something slithered in ahead of me and I had to follow that motherfucker in, listening for snakes in the 6 mil.

Got sewage in my shoes and soaked my favorite crawl suit in it. Busted main drain. Gray goopy water.

No D8 with Da

2

My oldest daughter is 13. She says, "The Prius smells like crawl." She says, "crawl space is the most literal word there is. It's the place where you crawl."

"Correct."

I spend a few hours a day on my hands and knees under homes, crawling through crawl spaces.

My oldest daughter has known about crawl spaces ever since I started working in crawl spaces. If she ever has a house that's failing, I don't want her to argue with reality over it.

When I told her how I found out about crawl spaces she laughed.

"The curse of. . .What was his dad's name?"

"What do you mean?"

"Sylvia Plath died of suicide. Her son died of suicide. Someone called it The Curse of Plath. I've been researching curses. You're probably cursed." My oldest daughter goes through phases. When she was younger, it was *Hamilton.* After that, Taylor Swift. These days, she reads Ottessa Moshfegh. She crochets and has an electric guitar. And, obviously, she researches curses.

"The guy didn't die of suicide," I said. "He died in a crawl space. We're talking about two different things."

"But that's not how curses work. It's not always identical fates. What was his name?"

"Why?"

"So, we can name the curse."

I don't remember the father's last name. But his first name was Juan Pablo. His death was in the paper. Juan Pablo Something or Other.

"Does it gross you out?" I asked my daughter. "The car? The smell?"

My oldest daughter held her nose. "I'll blame the Curse of Juan Pablo, and I can't really tell."

I can't always tell either. Some crawl spaces smell exactly like sandalwood, and sandalwood is a scent people pay for.

Old smells have strange lives.

The boy I met in summer school—JP's son before JP died—he would've known the smell of crawl. If he's still alive, I bet it would remind him of his father to sit in damp grass by an open crawl door on a muggy spring day and smell the fetid air escaping.

People who work in crawls smell like crawls. Decay. Grime. Sewer leak. Every time the boy held JP, he smelled what my daughter smells in my car.

I was in summer school when I met JP's boy. I probably failed the class I was retaking.

I was in a program for either mentally retarded or emotionally disturbed students. I drew on my shoes a lot, and I liked to read and smoke weed. My teachers had me take my classwork to a room called *content mastery*—a sort of headquarters for morons—where I read my books and ignored my assignments.

I liked the idea of being well read and poorly educated.

The day after JP died, I helped his son write an essay about a shark biting his teacher in half.

"Have you ever seen a dead body?" I asked him.

At the time, I didn't know JP was dead. I just thought his son had a lame assignment—a one-page essay about his teacher on the beach. The deal was this: the kid's class was supposed to dissect frogs, and the teacher didn't want the kid to see all the little embalmed corpses, and it was the only thing she could think of before the students collected their lab materials. People lose their shit like that, and we lived on the coast.

I had absolutely no idea.

"Is she hot?" I asked when he told me his teacher's makeshift assignment.

"She's really old," the boy said. "Not hot. Just a teacher."

"Then let's have her eaten by a shark."

For a solid hour, we wrote an essay about an old, bit-in-half lady writhing on the beach as she bled out beneath a bleak sky, her eyes wild with fear, panicking and packing sand against her wounds to try to stop the bleeding. Occasionally screaming at the seagulls that ate bits of her body floating in the tide going, "Haw. Caw. Heeaw."

The poor kid. Can you fucking imagine?

Whenever I think about it, I tell my daughter, "Don't smoke weed. And don't help people with their homework."

"What?" she says.

"Don't smoke weed and don't help people with their homework."

"Those two things aren't even related. That's like saying don't eat in bed and don't fold your sister's laundry."

"You can fold your sister's laundry."

"But that's what it's like."

"Fine. Don't smoke weed and don't eat in the bed, and don't help people with their homework, but feel free to fold your little sister's laundry."

"I'm not going to fold her laundry."

"Then don't do the other things either."

"Why?"

"So you don't get a JP. Your curse crap has fucked me up. Yesterday I was under a house with a busted main drain, slopping around in the piss you're now sniffing." I keep my crawl suits in my Prius. I wash them once a week, in theory. Your clothes don't need to be clean for you to get in a crawl space. "If I'm cursed, I have to blame JP for the pipe."

"Exactly. I'm glad you're finally realizing."

"I'm not 'realizing' anything. I'm just casting blame. Yesterday, I was driving on the highway and there was a traffic jam in the opposite direction. The drivers were furious. I could see when I passed them. In their faces, y'know? Do you know what they were mad about?"

"The traffic jam," my oldest daughter tells me.

"No," I say. "They were mad about what *caused* the traffic jam. Some drivers blamed potholes and some drivers blamed 18 wheelers, and some drivers blamed texting, and some drivers blamed alcohol."

"I am sure there were some who didn't."

"Some drivers blamed women, and some drivers blamed men, and some drivers blamed the idea of women and the idea of men."

"Okay."

"For the traffic jam they blamed these things."

"I get it."

"Masks for the traffic jam, vaccines for the traffic jam, the war for the traffic jam. The blame swirled inside their minds. And they weren't trying to get it right. They were just trying to feel it. And they were just yelling at whatever they thought caused the accident."

"Is there a point?"

"The point is, if I was stuck in the traffic jam, I might have blamed JP."

"Wait? It's not my fault if you blame JP." My daughter picks up my phone and opens Spotify, but I make sure the volume on my stereo is at zero.

"Yes. Before you, I had never thought about blaming JP for anything. Before you, he was just a guy who died in a crawl."

"Wait. How often do people die doing what you do?"

I thought a moment. "He's the only one I know of."

"What do you think his son does?"

"For all I know he's a doctor."

"Definitely would have had a good college entrance essay."

"What?"

"Dear admissions committee. Some people come from happy homes, and some people come from broken homes, and some people come from homes that were broken by broken homes. Did the house fall on him?"

"I don't know. I was too afraid to go under it. Wouldn't have known what I was looking at anyway."

"A house divided cannot stand long. You see, a divided house killed my father."

"Are you quoting Lincoln? Why do they have you thinking about this already?"

"Then blah, blah, blah. Pain, pain, pain. So, I am applying for admission at Prestigious University so that I might learn to find a way to help heal the houses. To bring peace to the families. Justice. Blah, blah. And stuff like that. If you die at work," my daughter tells me, "I'll probably get into Columbia."

"I guess I'd rather you go there than Yale."

"Let's just lower the windows a crack?"

"It's like 20 degrees right now."

"It smells."

"Hold your nose and blame JP."

"Do you think it's punching down? The Curse of Juan Pablo?"

"It's not a real curse, and you can't really punch down from a puddle of piss in a crawl space."

"I don't know. A teeny tiny crack?"

"No. Don't smoke weed, don't eat in bed, don't help people with their homework and don't roll down your car window when it's 20 degrees outside. But feel free to. . ."

"I'm not folding her laundry."

"Then don't do those other things either."

"Monster," she says.

I turn up the radio. "I know," I say. "I'm the worst." I forgot that my daughter pulled up the music, and it's Taylor Swift and that's a weird type of music to try to say cool shit over. "And that's why." The music drolls. "Don't smoke weed. And don't help anyone with their homework. And don't work in crawl spaces."

"I'm rolling my window down," she says.

"I'd rather you didn't," I say, "20 degrees." I am dialing up the volume, and Taylor Swift is fucking bumping, and my daughter's window is already going down, and the cabin of my Prius is already freezing cold, and Taylor Swift is singing, "driving the getaway car."

"Still smells like pee," my daughter yells at me over the wind and Swift.

"Fucking, JP," I yell back at her.

CRAWL SPACE TEXT THREAD #1

Germ: How delicious would a human baby have to be for you to eat it?

Darby: What? How do you mean?

Cowboy Dan: When's the last time I ate?

Darby: Like, eating a human baby? Did a customer bring it up?

Cowboy Dan: And how is it cooked?

Germ: ...

Cowboy Dan: And am I under duress? Or do you mean like going to the market and buying raw baby wrapped in plastic? Face down on that yellow Styrofoam tray? I don't think I could cook raw baby. Is it already cooked?

Germ: It's cooked how you'd cook it. Like chicken wings are. It's just the way it is. And I just mean normal.

Cowboy Dan: Like, how delicious would a human baby need to be for me to go to a restaurant and order human baby?

Darby: You boys need Jesus.

Cowboy Dan: Octopuses are supposed to be smart as shit. I've eaten those plenty. I would not call them delicious. Kind of rubbery. They'd have to be a ton better than octopus.

Darby: Do more church. Also, get on the other thread and post sales. I'm gonna explode. It's fucking leg day. I hate leg day. I wouldn't eat baby. Post sales.

Cowboy Dan: Just looked em up. They use tools. Do you think there are Octopus Unions? I don't think I can eat octopus again.

Germ: Babies don't use tools, and I doubt they're rubbery. It'd be like veal, wouldn't it?

Cowboy Dan: What color is it?

Darby: Whoa. Time out. Time.

Cowboy Dan: I'm not allowed to ask that?

Darby: No. You are not allowed to ask that. Look in your field manual. I think.

Cowboy Dan: Well I don't know, man. I feel like I'd rather eat a white baby. Is that better or worse?

Darby: Well hang on. CD, what are you?

Cowboy Dan: My mother was a botanist and my father worked railroad. I'd be a boat captain if I didn't always get so seasick. That's what they wanted for me. I'm under a house right now, but I am half underwater. We should hire an Octopus. My headlamp is dying.

Germ: Yeah. I was thinking more along the lines of, like, from other countries. I didn't even think about it being an American baby. Would they all cost different? Would there be organic ones?

Kipler: Poor white American babies would be cheap as shit, so long as you were in America.

Darby: Who tagged Kipler?

Kipler: Supply and demand. More poor white babies in America than any other type of baby.

Cowboy Dan: I don't know. I think there would be other factors at play. Marbleization, for one.

Germ: I couldn't do it. Not unless American babies were as delicious as shit.

Cowboy Dan: Don't eat shit, Germ.

Germ: . . .

Darby: . . .

Kipler: . . .

Cowboy Dan: If it sounds bad don't do it.

3

It always feels like the worst foundations are under the homes that don't look like they should have bad foundations.

It's usually simple. There are only a few different types of people who work in crawls, and there are only a few different types of bad foundations.

Everyone who works in crawl spaces has either done it forever, just got into the game, or can't find out how to break free. They are lost or ancient or looking around. They aren't stupid, but how could they be "smart"? They are 100% honest or 100% full of shit, or so uncertain that they themselves couldn't tell you. Some are fat. Some are skinny. Some tall. Some short. They either own guns and like showing them to you, or they'll say, "I wouldn't let you get to it," when they see a man wearing a gun in the wild. Others drop their gaze: "I can't own a gun," they'll tell you, "I might fall off the wagon and blow out my brains."

Sometimes my customers will ask, "What kind of person would work in a crawl space?"

"The installers or me?"

"Well, what's the difference?" This conversation will usually happen at the kitchen table. We'll be sitting there with my iPad looking at pictures from the crawl space below. Mold and muck and filth that needs to be wiped up and dragged away.

It's a good question.

"The difference? Usually, the inspectors liked school a little more and the installers can usually beat up the inspectors. Not that they would. They're good dudes. But a man who works all day digging in a crawl space will fist fight if it seems right. The installers have to be able to measure, lift, cut, mix, dig, crawl, follow work orders, collect payments. Manage the job site. Inspectors have to measure, crawl, diagram, diagnose, educate, communicate, follow up, and schedule business. Both installers and inspectors have to understand homes and drainage, and they have to be able to drag themselves through shitty situations."

"You've thought about it a lot."

"I drive all day. It's what I do when I'm not crawling. From house to house. All over Indiana. I wish I liked podcasts more. I mainly just listen to my own brain and talk to Imagination Mary Louise Kelly."

"I couldn't do it. I couldn't work in a crawl space. I can't even get in my own. It's terrifying."

"It takes a special kind."

I'm going to tell you about four inspectors, but I won't say much about the rest. All crawl space people are interesting, but most crawl space people aren't enjoyable. I cannot tell you about the installers because I have never installed. When my back was good enough to be an installer, I was a line cook. Then I was a college lecturer. Now I am a crawl space inspector. I've done a lot of jobs. I have no idea what the future holds.

Germ: the noobs in the crawl space industry are out to make money. You can earn a decent living selling any construction, and crawl salespeople can easily make six figures. They can also easily make exactly nothing. It's a 100% commission job.

When Germ started, I'd been inspecting a year. He had tremendous energy. He came over in the great resignation. I wandered over a little before that.

It works like this for new recruits: they know nothing other than they are hungry, humble, and smart. They can draw in CAD or can learn in a day. They have people skills and can communicate well over the phone, in person, via email and via text. They have a valid driver's license. They will get inside a crawl space.

Germ came from teaching middle school. He wanted to

be a wrestling coach. He wrestled for a Division II school I can't remember the name of.

He could never figure out how to coach. He wanted to hit the kids.

They were little shits. They couldn't make weight. They didn't know how to sacrifice. They talked when they should be quiet and didn't say anything when you asked them a question.

And then came the pandemic, and he answered a job ad because he didn't want to go back.

"Have you ever been in a crawl space, eh?" our Canadian boss Mortimer asked him during his interview. "Tight, confined work areas, eh? Gross. Dirty. Cobwebs and all manner of critters, y'know? Fine with you? Smells? You're fine with smells?"

"I'll wear a mask," Germ said. "I'll learn to like them," and he was hired.

He is single. He is shifty. He's 27 and still in love with his high-school sweetheart. They live in the same county. She is married and drives a brand-new high-trim black Chevy Tahoe with a personalized license plate that says: *MzTakn*.

Sometimes Germ drives by her house for no reason. He thinks to himself, "With my new job. . ."

He wants to fix it. He'd like her back bad. Every so often, he watches the movie *The Notebook.*

Darby: You have to feel sorry for the Darby's of this world. They are just optimistic enough to drive themselves crazy working for a better future.

Darby wasn't born into the crawl industry, he got roped into it after his time in the Navy.

He was a firefighter or worked on planes that refueled other planes. He didn't have PTSD.

He's been an installer, and he's run a crew, and he never went to college, because it's a waste of money.

"I make more money than anyone with a degree I know."

Once, he was a top salesperson, but he's gotten dragged into a quasi-administrative position. He is part teacher, part motivator, part big-brother figure to the whole sales force—even the older men.

His job is vindication. When he was 18, he enlisted. When he was 24 he started on crawls.

And hasn't it paid off? Haven't his college-educated friends asked for jobs? Aren't his college-educated friends jealous of his money?

So why?

Why can't it just feel right?

His girlfriends keep bringing up his drinking.

Breakfast beer doesn't interfere with his job.

It's worth it. He's working. It's worth it. His job.

> **Kipler:** There is a Kipler on every team. He always has about 100 college credits that he accumulated in the span of eight years, and he usually studied something like philosophy, and every time he flunked out—because he couldn't get to classes, he'll tell you, not because he wasn't smart—he would go back to work for his uncle in construction.

> He never ran a crew, but he could have if he wanted to, he'll say.

> He is married, shockingly.

> His wife is adorable, shockingly.

> After every time you talk to him, you get the suspicion that Kipler has an alt-right blog somewhere.

He loves Jordan Peterson and statistics about white people, and he'll say things like "lame-stream media" and "all lives matter," and he gets red-faced furious when he sees strangers alone in their cars wearing pandemic masks.

Cowboy Dan: Lo, there is a legend in all professions. A strange ancient creature who seems to be both unborn and eternal.

Cowboy Dan, perhaps reanimated. Anywhere from 60 to 4,000,000,000 years old. If he was unearthed from a crypt that was later found to be the first-ever crawl space, you wouldn't be surprised.

He wears a leather cowboy hat and alligator-skin boots.

He seems shrouded in secrets, but he's quick to share his memories. Often, he has toothpicks.

He rattles and patters and maybe everything he says is a lie. I'd bet he owns a few bull whips and smokes pipe tobacco, but men like him are, perhaps, never fully revealed to us.

We have weekly sales meetings. Darby runs them unless the Canadian Boss is in town.

The morning after my daughter brought up college admissions essays, I turned to Cowboy Dan in our little sales office and kind of whispered: "Have you heard of many people dying doing this? Like, how many crawl people do you know who've died in crawls?"

Our sales office smells like concrete dust and is filthy with fluorescent light and air-conditioned air. You sit brightly freezing in the smell of new construction.

Cowboy Dan smiled, cleared his throat, touched the leather brim of his cowboy hat. "Seeing ghosts in the laser?" he asked me.

"What?" We use lasers to determine foundation failure. I'll tell you more later, but mine is a Hilti Green Dot Self-Leveling laser and it shoots a green beam. It'll either focus on one spot and be a dot, or it spins around and around, sort of strobing a laser line in a 360. They show you where things used to be before they settled or bowed.

"Every crawl man has done it," Cowboy Dan said. Set up your laser in enough crawls and you'll start talking to the light. You'll start seeing the ghosts of old crawl men moving in the dust motes. They'll talk to you, and if you don't answer back it'll haunt you forever."

"I don't do that. What?"

Cowboy Dan showed me his ancient, browning teeth. His lips were chapped and falling apart, and he ran his tongue across them. "You will, though." He considered me as an elder would consider a baby. "It's written in the universe. Down in the quantum particles of it. Dancing in the quantum fields."

"The quantum what?"

"Google it," said Cowboy Dan. "The quantum level."

It's hard to say what makes someone good at selling crawl repair.

It doesn't always make sense.

It's the same with houses.

From the curb some houses seem fine. A human being walked through them and thought: I should live my life in this! But you get under them and you realize it'd be best to set the whole thing on fire. Let flames take to the earth what was yanked from the earth.

Every so often you get called out to some late 19th-century relic like an aching ruin from a Robert Lowell poem:

> Thirsting for
> the hierarchic privacy
> of Queen Victoria's century,
> she buys up all
> the eyesores facing her shore,
> and lets them fall.

But underneath, somehow, they are solid structures. The walls don't bow. The carpentry package isn't moldy. No standing, gray-shimmering water. No fortresses of cobwebs and the desiccated creatures captured and cocooned in the lurching air—filthy with dust motes swirling. No raccoon shit or raccoons in their little shredded newspaper nests, or snakes slithering in the Visqueen or snake skins shed in the folds.

Rats? No. Bats? No.

No blatant decay.

No nooks so tight your ribs get pinned between the greasy, foul earth and the mucus of whatever you're sliding under—sweaty ducts, rusted pipes, beams with termite tunnels so degraded you can yank hunks of wood from them like shredded wheat. No flittering sounds. "What is it?" No sewage. No brave cave crickets that spring at your face and get in your pants. Fingers crossed no wet hanging insulation that drags across the back of your neck as you move forth on hands and knees. Fingers crossed no fucking snakes. Fingers crossed the whole thing isn't viscous like an oyster, foul like a dead tooth, yellow and orange with bizarre mold growth, quivering with coming catastrophe.

There is no mistaking a shit show. You don't even have to understand how a home is constructed. You don't need to know what a footer is. A stem wall. A main beam. A joist. Sill plate. Band board. Subfloor. What is and isn't a permanent wood foundation.

Those—the permanent wood ones—Christ what fools. Say

it out loud: I will build my house on a foundation of treated wood.

I was in Carmel a year ago in the worst wood foundation I've ever seen. I got called out by an electrical engineer.

He was married and had a young child, and he and his family had moved into their home a few months before. It cost them $300k.

Carmel, Indiana is the Tesla, traffic circle, and Country Club suburb of Indianapolis. It feels like debt and marital strife. It's bright fresh, white concrete roads. The men aspire to be Elon Musk. The women aspire to be Gwyneth Paltrow if they're skinny, Kim Kardashian if they're thick. Everyone in Carmel, Indiana will die in a hospital. They'll die of something like addiction or cancer.

"I've been in the crawl," the engineer told me, "but I don't know what I'm looking at."

I wanted to say, "Me either, muffin fluffer. Houses aren't built like this." But you have to stay professional.

He had memorable teeth. I can't even remember if he had hair. Just teeth, teeth, teeth.

When I told him about his house, his wife was sitting at the table with us. She was holding her newborn baby. Maybe the child was adopted. It felt like the engineer and his wife didn't really have sex. Maybe once a season, but only with the lights off. Quickly. No talking afterward. Emily Dickinson energy. Only halfway rhyming.

> Carmel, Indiana sex.
>   Low carb alcohol.
> If it's a boy we'll –
>   Call it Braxton sex.
> Our couch is from Costco.

"I don't care if it costs 20 grand. I just don't want to think about it again," the wife said, "It's stressful having a bad foundation." At night, she'd lay in bed worrying if everything would collapse. Her marriage. Her home. Her baby. Nothing left but a diaper of dust.

The engineer wanted to murder his wife when she brought up money. He pointed his teeth at her. If I wasn't there, he might have screamed. "We don't even know what it is yet."

"We know it's not good," the wife said.

"It's not," I agreed. "It's pretty bad."

The baby started crying. I don't remember everything. I showed them pictures of all the rot they lived on. I had crawled the sloppy perimeter of the home's foundation wall, and every piece of wood was black and crumbling, and every ounce of home we sat in rested on that rot. Some engineer at some university had determined that treated wood wouldn't do what it was doing so long as everything went as planned, but, as is so often the case, the plan fell the fuck apart.

"But it's not going to be like 20 grand, is it?" the engineer asked. If only he could use those teeth to gnaw something off and go free. I would respect him more if he was missing a hand and dashing somewhere with a mouthful of his own blood.

"You could probably sue someone for how this house was built." When I'm working with white families in Carmel, I just tell them how shitty everything is so they know they might have to call their parents.

I can't remember exactly what all they did, but they didn't do enough. They might never sink through the floor when binging Netflix, but I didn't promise them that. No one ever could.

The only way the wife will ever have peace of mind is if their house burns down by accident and the engineer is inside when it happens.

You can imagine her holding her baby and scraping through the ashes to try to find the engineer's teeth. Like once she finds them, she can finally be free.

PARTS OF CRAWL SPACE FOUNDATION

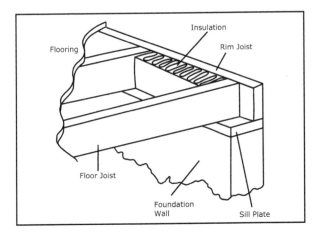

4

I hope my wife never looks for my teeth in a pile of ash, but I do own an ancient house that has more issues than I care to share. It's overwhelming. We are old-house people. Nothing we have sits on a level surface, and everything we own smells like us.

My oldest daughter says, "Have you heard of nepotism babies? I wish I was a nepotism baby."

"A what?"

"You know. Nepotism. Like, if your parents are rich and famous so you're rich and famous."

It was a Saturday, and the sun was out and we were walking through the cemetery near our house looking at gravestones, because my wife will send us on walks if we seem depressed, but she doesn't tell us where we should go, so we were standing in front of a gravestone that said:

Beulah Chambers
1898 – 1910

"That's young," I said. "Think she was a nepotism baby?"

My daughter spends a moment watching the grave. "Hard telling. Do you think she picked her own tombstone? Or do you think it was picked for her?"

"Are you gonna need a lot of therapy someday?"

"You would choose between fonts, right? Like it's a Google Slide."

"Probably. You'd think they'd have like a book of fonts you could choose from. I wonder if it's the same salesperson for the casket and headstone?"

"What do 12-year-olds regret?"

"You'd know better than me. But in 1910? Who knows? Not winning a ribbon at some fair for raising the cutest speckled pig? Losing a bracelet?"

Beulah Chambers' gravestone sat amongst several Chambers. Harold Chambers, presumably her father, died in

1919. Angelica Chambers, presumably her mom, died in 1932. None of their tombstones matched.

We wandered off through the cemetery, making up lives to go along with people's names. The granite markers twinkled in the cold sunlight, and the air smelled of cut grass. There were geese near the creek that strode alongside the cemetery. They went: honk, honk, hee-yonk.

An old man with a walker came scuffing down the asphalt path that ran between the creek and the cemetery, and a few of the ornery geese lifted their wings in defiance and began to challenge up to him—their tongues curled in their open beaks as they hissed.

The old man froze, his knobby hands peaked against the handles of his walker, his eyes wide saying, "Shoo." He was afraid he'd trip over the geese. You could see it in his face. He looked from his feet to the geese to the ground. "Get. Get." Fear in his body, face, voice, and eyes.

My daughter and I jogged up to help, and I kicked at one of the geese, and they backed off toward the creek, wings flapping—loose feathers floating willy-nilly.

"Damn birds," the old man said. He looked misplaced but wore it gently. His last defense mechanism—kindness in the eyes. "Saved," he said and shook his head—the geese hee-yonking away. "Can you imagine a sillier way to die?"

"Slipping on a banana peel," my daughter said. She was brushing her hair away from her eyes.

"Even better," said the old man. "Y'all leaving already? I mean, it's a popular place." He looked toward the cemetery. "People are just dying to get in here."

"We're meandering," I said. "Passing the time."

"Understood. I'm 82 and don't know a single person buried here. I think I just come to scare myself, but not like that. Not with the geese. With the graves, you know? With the mortality." He motioned to the cemetery. "With the permanence of it. The absolute finality." He seemed lost a moment in thought—yearning toward infinity. He eased his attention toward us. "Walk with me until I'm less afraid of the birds?"

We didn't need to be anywhere, so we strolled up the asphalt walkway—the old man moving gingerly. We watched him alongside us, shielding him from nothing. His walker dictated our pace, his crinkled face bunched around his eyes—squinting in the sun—his ancient hands clamped down, half shaking.

"My name's Harvey," the old man said.

"That's my father's middle name," I told him.

"I wish it was mine. Or I wish I had another first name. Or a middle I could use. I liked it as a kid. Then there was that movie. A giant invisible rabbit that only a drunk could see. The rabbit was named Harvey. After that, when people said my name, I could hear them calling me that invisible rabbit. Does that make sense? Like, they said my name, but they meant that movie."

"Jimmy Stewart?"

"Yeah," said Harvey, "but he wasn't the rabbit."

We neared a few graves, and Harvey dragged up to one. He froze. Looked around. "What the fuck was I doing?" he said, then mumbled a bit of nothing. His eyes widened. "Sorry. I cuss some. It's not normal. My neighbor thinks it's a symptom. Says I should talk to my doctor. What would he do? Brush my teeth with soap?"

Harvey leaned toward one of the graves. There was a small bouquet of white lilies on the ground near a headstone. They looked a few days old—the edges of the petals the same color as wet cigarettes. He stretched at the lilies but couldn't quite reach, his outstretched fingers trembled toward the stems.

Harvey looked at me. "Can your daughter help?"

"Steal flowers?"

"Look at the name." The name on the gravestone was Archibald Cumberfletch. "He deserves to be stole from."

My daughter didn't wait for my reply, said, "Just a few, or the whole bouquet?"

"Even better," Harvey said. "Grab 'am all."

She fetched the flowers in a quick lowering motion, shrugged her shoulders at me, and we moved along, Harvey's feet dragging against the asphalt and my daughter carrying the stolen flowers, moving glacially toward wherever.

"Do you work?" Harvey asked. "I heard on TV a lot of people don't work anymore. I don't blame them. Occupations are soul sucking."

"I inspect houses," I said. "Foundations."

"Where do you do that?"

"All over Indiana. Wherever there are houses, I get under them."

"I can't take this," Harvey said, and he stepped away from his walker, touched the handle of it once or twice when he was clear, just to steady himself, and then he wobbled down a row of graves. "We have to walk over bodies to get there." Harvey glanced at my daughter then gave his full attention to traversing the uneven grass.

"It's fine," my oldest daughter said. She looked at me and mouthed the word, "therapy," but Harvey didn't see. We were following him simply because he was walking away.

Harvey stopped and stood in front of a gravestone—a simple shape carved from damp-looking concrete with a name banner on the top and a life-span banner on the bottom that had been chiseled out so you couldn't read them.

He held his hand toward my daughter. "Flowers," he said, and my daughter handed him the lilies and Harvey set them against the headstone and brushed the petals with the back of his fingers.

"Whose is this?" I asked.

Harvey watched me. He looked back at the grave. "I don't know. Are you able to read it?"

"No, but. . ."

"Oh, thank god," said Harvey. "I've come to this grave at least 100 times. I don't know what I'd do if other people could just read the name."

"Have you asked anyone?"

"The cemetery people know the story," said Harvey. "But they can't or won't tell. I offered them twenty dollars. They literally laughed at me. Twenty dollars was a lot of money in my day. But I'm not offering anyone more than that for just a bit of information. Like, if I give you twenty dollars, and you don't at least put something in my hand, I feel cheated."

"You've come here a hundred times?" my daughter said. "And every time you get it flowers?"

"Of course not," said Harvey. "I don't *get it* flowers. I borrow it flowers. Today from Archibald Cumberfletch. Some other time from Pinkerton Snoot. A lot. I don't know. It seems weird to go to the store to buy brand new flowers when there are all these laying around not being used." He motioned to the graveyard, at all the bouquets scattered throughout the grave markers.

"Do you only steal flowers from people with names like that?" I asked.

"Names like what?"

"I don't know. Names that sound . . ."

"Prim and goofy?"

"I guess."

"I try to. I guess it's backwards sometimes. If I see a name like that, I take its flowers and bring them here. If I think about the grave, I'll go find it flowers. The names I take from could be anything. No matter who I take from, it seems there's always more."

"What's your last name?" my daughter said. "Would you steal flowers from yourself?"

"Harvey Corker?" Harvey said. "If I saw that carved in stone, I'd probably steal the flowers and scratch out the name and piss on the earth. But I don't think it sounds prim. It just sounds like an asshole."

"Don't worry," I said to Harvey. "Most people don't see their own graves. I mean, you'd have to die before yourself."

"I wouldn't be against it," Harvey said, and he directed our attention back to the grave. "I used to think maybe the mason didn't get paid for making the tombstone, but I feel like if that was the case, he would've just taken the whole stone back and used it for someone else. My current theory is that it was revenge. Who wouldn't like to scratch out a name or two?"

We stood quietly, and I could feel Harvey cooking up theories and scenarios to explain the nameless grave to himself, and I looked over at my oldest daughter and I could tell she was bored.

"Are you still afraid of the geese?" I asked, and Harvey was pulled back into the moment and he looked around the cemetery, a kind of proudness on his face, his shoulders kind of pulled back.

"I don't think so," he said. "I guess there's only one way to know for sure. But I'll probably try to just stay away from them."

I motioned at my daughter. "Her mother will want her home soon."

"Of course," said Harvey. "Of course."

"I hope you figure it out," said my daughter.

"Figure it out?"

"Yeah. About the name."

"Oh, that won't happen," said Harvey. "I'm 84 years old, and I can't remember figuring out anything."

"Then good luck with the geese," I said, and my daughter and I began to walk home, and the last time I looked back, Harvey was still watching the grave, still just standing there.

5

It was Monday morning at 6:51 AM, and, like all Monday mornings, I was sitting in the sales office. The goddamned cold and the goddamned cement dust and the fluorescent, fluorescent, fluorescent light, and I had had about 9 cups of coffee, and I was probably going to have about 9 more, and Germ asked, "Does Delta-8 come up in drug tests?"

None of the real bosses were there yet. I had a stain on my shirt, so I was cursing JP and picking at the stain, and my shirt was black, and I think it was old toothpaste. Had I drooled on myself because of a curse?

"Christ," said Darby. He was standing up at the podium in front of the office. We were there to update our Key Performance Indicators, and check in with our foremen, and get trained and teased and harassed and taunted.

Our company culture was based on the teachings of some famous American soldier and completely extreme. We had slogans and mantras and incantations that we would regurgitate in allegiance, and it was as demoralizing as you can imagine—we read posters off the wall to each other like they were Psalms:

And lo, we shall pulleth our boots on daily,

Lest we march eternally barefooted into the furnace of damnation.

"Technically," said Darby, "I'm supposed to keep records when I hear shit like that. Like that Delta-8 shit, but Germ's new, and maybe we didn't cover drug usage during training. Let's use it as a teachable moment for the whole team," Darby looked up from his computer. "Don't do drugs. Don't talk about drugs." Darby's eyes were glassy red. He might have already had beers. He blinked aggressively, like he was using his eyelids to crush cans.

"Delta 8 isn't a drug," said Germ. "They sell it at the gas station. It's legal."

Kipler heard the word 'legal' and his head sprung into action and his mouth gaped open and he barked his way into the conversation. "Currently," he said. "But don't be an idiot. They're collecting data. We'll see. I bet they tax the hell out of it."

"No one in here does Delta-8," I said. "Or real weed either." I looked around the room. "Guys?"

"Fuck weed," said a few of the guys. Personally, I was fairly stoned—I can't drink but I still get high, and the only way I could tolerate my Monday sunrise meeting was to eat a low-milligram edible before my drive to the office—but lying to your assistant manager about drugs is what you're supposed to do.

"Thank you," Darby said, and he pointed at me. "Top guy things. What's that on your shirt?"

Top guy things were the things top guys did. But you didn't become a top guy by doing top guy things. The things you did just became top guy things when you sold a lot of jobs. Darby didn't know it yet, but that month, I hadn't sold shit. My KPI were garbage. Average dollars per lead: down. Average dollars per sale: down. Closing rate: dogshit. Embarrassing. Double digits, but not by much.

We were set up as a one-call close operation. We were supposed to inspect a home, present findings, discuss a proposal, and sign-up business the first visit. We had endless meetings about closing percentage. We practiced overcoming objections religiously. It became instinctual. Built into us. The new guys would call each other on the phone after missing out on a sale to rehearse.

"Bro, listen to this, bro." And they'd dive into the minutiae of their appointment. What personality type the customer had, what kind of home? What type of work they were having done? What it cost? Who you bid against? Who was still coming? Who came before?

"Were there dishes in the sink?"

"What does that matter?"

"Are you kidding me? You don't look for dishes?"

"Why?"

"If there's dishes in the sink you don't bring up warranties and you don't bring up relative humidity and you don't bring up how many amps the sump pump pulls or interest rates on financing, or AP fucking R. Just show them the pictures of all the funky shit and cobwebs. Hopefully there's a dead rat. I found a dog skeleton once. Did I ever tell you I found a dog skeleton? It was on a shelf. Like somebody put it there to die."

"If there's dishes in the sink, the crawl's bound to be a shit show. Is that it?"

"That's the stupidest thing you've ever said. It has nothing to do with that."

"Then what's the point?"

"The point is that people who wait to wash dishes do not give a fuck about specifics. All they are is emotions."

"Bro?"

"If they got clean sinks, they want specifics. Dirty sink people don't care about details. Same thing with cats. If someone has cats, all they want you to do is talk to them about their cats. They'll buy from you if they like you. Keep them busy. Get out your laser level and set it up in their living room and let it whirl and madden the cats, and while the customers are watching their cats spin in circles chasing lasers, just start handing them things to sign."

There were scripts and talk tracks and personality assessments. It became rote.

If, after we presented a price and asked for a signature, a customer said:

"I need a few days to think about it."

We would seek to clarify and restate:

Lean back. "Mr. or Mrs. Homeowner, I understand that you need a few days to think about it. Out of curiosity, during those few days, what are the main things you'll be thinking about?"

They always thought about the same thing: "Money, I guess. It's just that it's a lot of money."

"Okay, so you're comfortable with the company, you're comfortable with the solution, you're just concerned about price. Correct?"

"Correct."

That's an isolation close. You get your customer to agree with you on a single point of contention.

Then you redirect and satisfy:

"I understand. It's not a small investment. If it was less money, you probably wouldn't even need to think about it at all."

"Exactly," the customer says. "I mean, I know it needs to get done."

Wait. Listen. Silence is musical. It holds the rhythm of every nearby heart and brain. It is energy inside energy. It is light inside light. And there is more information in silence than there is information in the spoken truth. Possibilities are always infinite, so at a point in time, the silence will produce the possibility you want. It is fleeting, but it is always there. In the fabric of every moment is a route to your answer. You can only find something when you're looking for it. When it is time, and only you can know when it is time, you say: "How about I work on the price." Concentrate. Type on your laptop. Use a calculator. Chew on your bottom lip a tiny bit and mutter some numbers at yourself. Whatever it needs to be. Then: "How about I drop the price to (lower number) and we just get you on the schedule today?"

Then shh. If the customer never speaks again, you never speak again. If they sit at their table with their mouth shut until the plaster starts dropping from the ceiling and the coming civil war marches through their front yard, you don't say shit until after the swords are beaten back into plowshares.

Hopefully you got them. If they don't sign up, you do it all over again or try to get them prequalified for financing. If that doesn't work put all your things away, but don't leave. Keep talking. Wait a while. Try again. Your feet are booted, they will not be incinerated by the fires of hell.

Of course, everything is easy on paper, and I was in an epic sales slump. Some people would blame themselves, or lead flow, or the crawl gods. I blamed JP. Ghost-ass motherfucker.

I had two weeks to turn it around or I was going to have to go to Ohio. My numbers were usually strong, but that month,

I wasn't feeling it. Sometimes, you just underperform and fuck shit up. Even bald eagles probably run into clean building windows on occasion, regally.

One of our corporate mottos was:

Never Underperform

Another was:

Embrace the Pain

To me, embracing the pain did not seem like a top-guy thing.

Kipler couldn't let Delta 8 go. "But if people in here did do that," he pretended to smoke an invisible joint in a 1990s high school kind of way, "they should smoke illegal weed instead. Every time you get the corner-store shit, you're just making the government stronger."

"Have any of y'all even talked to your foremen?" Darby said. He stood trembling at the podium, behind his laptop. His eyes glowed tiny reflections of his computer screen at us. "We're not here to talk about weed or the government or delta whoever."

"I Googled it," said Cowboy Dan. He was sitting in the back with his cowboy hat pulled tight toward his eyes and his phone about three inches from his face. "There's an article. Delta 8. Dah. Dah. Dah." He scrolled a while on his phone and kept saying dah, dah, dah, dah as he scrolled. "Fuck it. Too long. Who gives a shit?" He set the phone down. "Don't get hurt and they won't ever drug test you."

"Fuck, guys," said Darby. "Go talk to your goddamned foremen."

"Hell no," said Kipler. "Whoever's putting in today's job will want to murder me. It's a shit show. Really, they should probably just knock the house down."

"Then why'd you sell it?"

"To hit goal."

Darby considered it. "Fair."

I can't tell you the name of the company where I was working, because I probably signed some kind of non-disclosure agreement, and, besides, I don't work there anymore, and I think most of the men I worked with have since moved on. In hindsight, you could have probably looked around the room and seen the signs. Most things happen gradually.

A foundation wall, for instance, breaks in stages.

First, it cracks horizontally. This usually happens one or two blocks down from the top of your foundation. If you have a basement, and the walls aren't finished (usually drywall), then your basement probably looks like this:

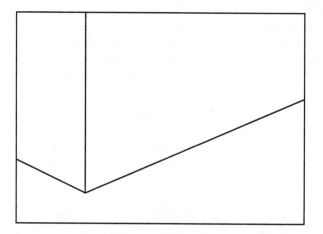

When a wall begins to fail, you usually get separation between the second and third row of block, which looks like this:

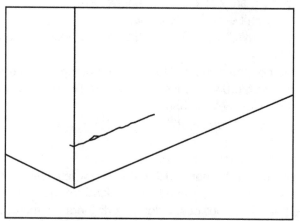

Once that crack has been established, the wall begins to really push in, and the cracks begin to run from the top to the bottom of the wall. That leads to stair step cracking, which looks like this:

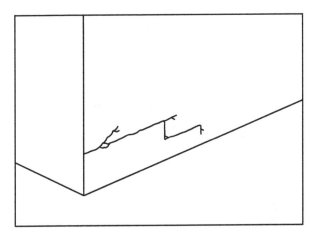

Then the wall begins to sheer—to separate, to pull apart:

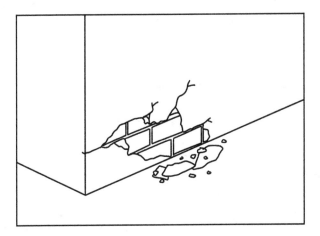

After that, it's absolute failure:

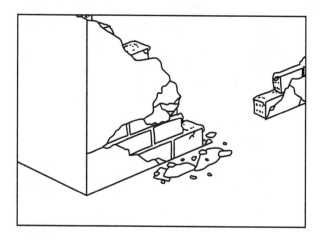

If you see cracks in the wall, you can go ahead and assume someday you'll have to repair them. The later in the stages, the sooner you should do it, and home repair always gets more expensive, because here is how you calculate for the price of a job. You take the cost of your labor plus the cost of your materials and that number is 40% of the price tag, because you have to shoot for 60% gross profit. The equation looks like this:

(labor + materials) / .4 = price of your job

and wages should always go up. So, home repair is always more expensive in the future.

Also, it's impossible to predict when the wall will move from one stage to the next. You can only know where it is in the process. Once it's gone too far, it's over. Once it starts, it never stops on its own. Crack. Creak. Snap. Crumble.

"Alright, men," said Darby. He was dallying with his laptop and the projectors were projecting. They never dimmed the overhead lights. Light stacked atop light. "Here in a second, Mortimer's gonna call in from Canada." Mortimer was the real boss who was sequestered in Canada because he feared covid and Americans. All of us moved in and out of houses daily, in the thick of the pandemic, deeper in someone's breath than you can be in someone's breath. In their homes where they boasted, quarreled, loved, laughed, screamed, hocked loogies and snored.

A quarter of us had been downed by the Vids at one time or another. I caught it bad after a company breakfast and nearly lost my job because I couldn't run an appointment for two weeks. They had me call phone lists with a 103-degree fever trying to scrape together follow-up sales and hit goal.

Mortimer would text me from Canada: Keep grinding. I have faith in you.

I texted back: I'm in the emergency room.

Mortimer texted back: Why?

I texted back: To stay alive.

He texted back: That's the spirit.

I texted back: They might put me on a ventilator.

He texted back: Get plenty of rest and drink lots of fluids and make lots of calls and get me some sales.

I texted back: I can only do two of those three things at a time.

He texted back: Okay. Do the sales two first and then do the rest and fluids and don't let them put you on a ventilator. You got this.

I texted back: What I've got is covid.

He texted back: And even that can't get in the way of a top guy's goal.

Mortimer was on the screen, wearing a mask, being broadcast into the sales meeting by internet. Every day, you'd go to a home and visit a person with their mics turned off on meetings, listening to the dull chatter, and each of them were probably the Mortimers of their worlds. For every person on a Zoom call, there are 1,000 people out there balancing the internet on their backs. Making the internet from their sweat. Touching reality so their managers don't have to.

"Gentleman," Mortimer said. "Greetings from majestic

Canada."

His mouth was masked, but his eyes were smiling.

"Just been, eh, looking over the numbers then," his eyes un-smiled. "Not, eh, admirable. No. Not what I'd expect from this team, no." He touched his brow. "But before we get to the numbers." He picked up another sheet. "Have you guys, eh, heard of these things the pronouns? It's a new world, gentlemen, and I for one am here to embrace it. So, eh, we're gonna go around the room."

"Go around what?" said Kipler.

"The room," said Darby.

"I'd really rather we didn't," said Kipler.

"Who's that?" said Mortimer. "Darby, I couldn't make it out."

"It's nothing."

"No, no," said Mortimer. "HR told us there might be some pushback. I'm not sure they expected it this early in the exercise. I mean, I haven't even gotten to the objective."

"We know what the objective is," said Kipler. "You want to know how we self-identify."

"Is that?" Mortimer strained his eyes at his computer screen from the other end of the continent. "Kipler?" Mortimer waved at us through his camera. "I knew you wouldn't be quick to join in, Kipler. Always the thorn. Lovingly. I say it with love. It's a trait of the Americans. Shrewd tenacity, and I understand that change doesn't come easily. So, I'll start. I'm Mortimer. I'm from Canada. I, eh, work in the foundation industry. And I'm a he / him." Mortimer stared into his camera for a long time. "Easy enough, right? So, we're going to go around the room like always. Getting your monthly projections. Numbers so far are a little light, I can't lie. We've got 14 selling days left, gentlemen. . . "

"Gentlepeople," said Kipler.

Mortimer adjusted his mask. "Gentlepeople," he agreed. "And, to be clear, it's looking a little light. So, be honest. With your numbers. Because I am going to need to know. On the one hand, I am definitely going to need you gentlemen. . ."

"People."

"Gentlepeople, to dig deep. I have never missed a sales projection, and I don't intend to start now. So, gentlepeople," Mortimer said. "We'll start with Kipler there. So, just your name, your monthly projection, and your pronouns. If you would."

Kipler hung his head like his mother had cancer. "I'm Kipler," he said, because he needed the job and because he was one of those men who talked loud and pissed their pants when shit got real, "I should get to 80k." He took a deep huff. "I'm a he / him. Obviously."

"Oh, obviously," said Mortimer and he typed in Kipler's number and shared the screen to show an Excel document. He circled Kipler's projection endlessly with his mouse icon. "He / him," he said. "Eighty K." Circle circle circle. "Eighty k." Circle. "That's a little light, isn't it? Not top guy at all, is it?"

"Bad month. Bad leads."

"Just to be clear," said Mortimer. "That's Kipler. 80k. He / him. I get that right? Anything need to change?"

"Look, I'm hoping to hit 80, maybe I'll do more."

"Kipler. 80k," Mortimer clicked his tongue. "He / him. He says. What about you, Germ?"

The only reason any of us would talk to Germ was because he was having an epic launch to his one-call close career. He swam in the lunatic Kool-Aid of corporate cultism. We all hated him, but we were afraid he knew secret talk tracks to land a deal with, and we all wanted whatever magic he had to rub off on us.

"Germ. 250. He / him."

"That's more like it. That's a he / him all day long. Those are he / him numbers from Germ. 250. He / him. Let's fucking go."

I looked at Darby. Darby looked at me. I couldn't decide if Mortimer understood pronouns or was just an asshole. Sometimes, I thought he was autistic. With our eyes, Darby and I conveyed this to each other.

"Cowboy Dan," Mortimer said.

Cowboy Dan took off his hat and slicked back his greasy hair with a calloused palm. "Cowboy Dan. Cowboy. I'll sell what I'll sell once I sell it."

Mortimer began to enter Cowboy Dan's projection. "Dan. Cowboy. TBD. Numbers need to get a little better there though, partner. We can't carry you forever just because you've been here the whole time." Cowboy Dan was inherited from the location's history. He was the first person who had ever worked for the company, but the company had changed hands a half dozen times, and Mortimer and Darby were corporate elements from a new national-footprint company that had essentially bought Cowboy Dan when they bought the location. The CEO liked him because he was a good symbol of a commitment to continuity, but everyone else in the company treated him like he was the subject of a silver alert. The best part about Cowboy Dan is he didn't give a fuck.

"I love your accent, Mortimer," Cowboy Dan said. "It reminds me of Keebler Elves. Do they have those in Canada? They live in a tree and make cookies."

Then Mortimer sort of brightened up. "I almost forgot. Guys. . ."

"People," said Kipler.

"Next Monday is the big day!"

Mortimer had decided that we all need to know the team members better, and he had implemented a monthly presentation schedule. Each month, a member of the team had to get up at the podium and tell us their life story. We had drawn straws to see who went first and we figured Cowboy Dan had lost on purpose.

"You ready for that, Cowboy?" Mortimer asked.

"Hell, I could go right now," Cowboy Dan said. "Get it the fuck out the way. I need to borrow a laser for the second half though."

"No, no," said Mortimer. "We have to follow the schedule. And today is for pronouns and goals. Cook?" Mortimer said to me.

"Put me down for 50. Also, this isn't how this works."

"Fifty?!" said Mortimer. "I agree. It's now how it works. You're supposed to tell me what you think you'll have at the *end* of the month. Not what you have now."

Darby started looking at something on his phone.

"That's not what I have now. That's the projection. I'm a he / him. If I have zero or a bajillion or negative two. I might also be currently dealing with a curse of sorts, but I don't think that affects my pronouns."

"I mean, technically. But if you're only gonna have 50 at the end you might have to go be a he / him in Ohio. What do you have now?"

"Less than that. Someone died a long time ago, and my daughter says that's why my numbers are low. I think it's also how I got this stain." I pointed to my shirt. "I don't think she's right, but I definitely think about it."

"Fourteen selling days," said Darby.

"Cook. He / him. He says. He / him. He says. And he might be cursed." He typed some things. "Probably headed to Ohio."

We had gotten word from corporate that every branch had to send one of its top guys to Ohio to help get the place going. There were a dozen or so locations. Indiana. Florida. Michigan. Others. And, now, a newly acquired office in Ohio. They only trusted a few of us to go. Me. Cowboy Dan. Kipler. Four more inspectors I'd rather not tell you about, and whoever came in last in sales for the months was shipping out for a week to try and build a backlog of work for Ohio to get started installing.

I liked Ohio, but some states just seem like they'd have bad houses to get under. Back where I grew up in Texas there are scorpions and rattlesnakes and roaches. Fuck that a million percent. Get into a chamber, see a nest of rattlers, and then your headlamp blinks out. The smallest noise and you die of stroke and your body is slowly picked apart by cockroach mouths. The squirmy, brown bastards have babies in your brains. Long, brown quivering antennae dragging flimsily across your dead, open eyeballs.

Jesus, could JP have been bitten by a snake? No one there to suck out the poison? Shoved his head under an air duct and caught fangs to the face? Chomp! The venom speeding toward his heart and brain? Just listening to the rattlers rattle away through the crawl until the world faded?

"Two weeks," said Darby. He held up two fingers. "Hard reset and get grinding. Hit goal. And then you won't have to worry about Ohio. Fuck that curse."

"Fine," I said. "Put me down for 150," I said. "Fuck the curse."

"And your pronouns?" said Mortimer.

"I already told you. He / him."

"That's right," said Mortimer. "I sometimes forget." He typed something. "150," he said. "He," he said. "Him." He typed more. "Not cursed."

After that, we finished going around the room, giving our predictions and declaring our pronouns, and everyone was a he / him, and everyone who didn't have good enough predictions was asked to restate their pronouns a half dozen times, and the meeting wrapped up at 7:30 AM, and I felt like I had fluorescent light poisoning.

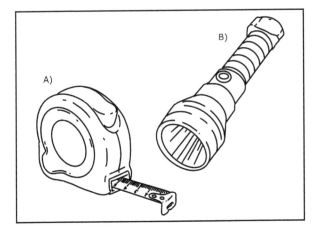

6

I said there are tools, but I haven't said what the tools are. The hardest part of my job is getting out of a house with everything I took into the house. I am constantly replacing something lost, and I don't always have time to get a good replacement. Many tools in my bag are subpar. They work, but just barely. Here is my current collection:

1. Light
You cannot do this job without a light. It is dark in the crawls. It can be scary. And I hate my current headlamp. It's a LUXPRO CUBI 738. It's a 362-lumen lamp with a max charge of 3.5 hours, but I feel like it works for about 30 minutes. I had a DanForce Ultrabright CREE 1080 lumen that held a good charge and threw a baller beam, but I smacked it getting into a crawl and now it's garbage. I liked it so much, I can't throw it out. It sits in my trunk, dead. I should replace it, and it's only $35, but I'm weird about money. I'll invest four dollars in a pack of gum and a diet soda three times a day, but I have a hard time spending $11 on anything I actually need.

Some guys use handheld flashlights, but it makes it a lot harder to take pictures—you've got one less hand.

An iPhone light does in a pinch, but it's not a good time. Especially if the crawl's a shit show.

An iPhone is like a 40-lumen light. I'm pretty sure that's about what you get with a Zippo lighter. And it feels like that if you're down in a crawl and have to use one. Like you're tunneling out of military prison in a film from 1954.

2. Distance
There are several lengths and distances you measure. The first thing I measure is the shape of the house. For that, I use a Crescent Lufkin Geardrive measuring wheel. It's a single 4" wheel at the end of a telescoping handle. You hold the handle, place the wheel against the ground, and walk. The wheel spins across the earth, the spinning takes the measurement which

shows on a counter at the base. You walk the perimeter of the house and draw the shape of the house from a bird's eye view.

The second thing I measure is the crawl space entrance, which is hopefully outside the house and not a trapdoor in a closet. For this, you need a tape measure, and you need this measurement for two reasons: the crew will need to know what they're getting into, and if you replace the door, you need to know the size. Some crawl doors are so tight, you feel like you're being born in reverse getting into them. You go feet first and wriggle quick, and your whole body moves like a corkscrew as you pack yourself deeper, stopping only once your head's underground. No matter how tight an entrance, leaving crawls feels like being reborn. You drag yourself out of a hole and into the light and your eyes sting in the sun.

I'm not super partial to any particular make or model of tape measure. I currently use a Craftsmen 25'. It's always best if the tape is numbered on both sides, and the wider the tape the better. Skinny tapes fold on accident. It's also best if it is self-retracting with a lock. But if you have it extended to a full 25', and you trip the lock to let it retract, slow the retracting tape with your thumb and forefinger, or it'll build up speed while it's retracting and the hook slot will smack the holy hell out of your hand.

Besides the door, you need a tape to measure from the dirt of the crawl floor to the base of a joist (you need at least 18" between the joist and the dirt or you have to dig out so the crews can work—on their bellies dragging dirt by hand). If you're doing any woodwork—replacing wet, degraded wood with good new wood—you'll need the size of the wood. The joists, sills, and beams.

You also need to know distances from walls to any proposed support systems, sizes of clearances, and locations of obstructions—air ducts, plumbing, electrical.

3. Humidity
When I'm doing my job well, I take a few different humidity reads. I do one in front of the house—to get a read on what

the outdoor air is—and I do several reads under the house to determine if humidity is an issue. Basically, humidity is an issue if your wood is reacting, but wood doesn't always react the same way to humidity. It depends on the wood. See, there's no such thing as just: wood. Wood is not like Lego blocks.

Different species have different properties. Beyond that, different aged trees have different properties. Beyond that, trees of the same species but from different places have different properties. And trees of the same age and species from the same location can be treated in different ways. Treating is how you prepare wood to be lumber.

You can dive as deep as you want into why wood is different. I have been in a crawl space where all the wood was from the same species, age, location, and had been treated, presumably, in the same manner. But of the 100 or so joists: four had mold on them.

You sit in the crawl staring up at the affected joists and just say: "Shit's baffling."

You can't remediate single joists. It's against best practice. If there is one moldy joist in your crawl space, you have to treat the entire crawl space to know that you have killed all the mold. If you don't treat the mold it will spread. If it spreads, your foundation gets worse and 50% of the air that gets in your crawl gets in your house. Mold in your crawl, mold in your house. Mold in your house, mold in your lungs. Mold in your lungs. . . allergies, irritation, cancer.

I mean, not always, but. . .

When I was in my 20s, I worked for a water damage expert in South Texas putting together water damage reports. Back then, you could get insurance companies to cover mold remediation. Today, they really won't cover anything foundation related.

If someone else is paying for it, or it doesn't cause you too much financial strife to cover the project, I'd say do a full solution every time—drainage, encapsulation, mold remediation, a dehumidifier.

But you can't look up the way the other 96 joists in a crawl space will respond to their environment in the future. So, if I come out to your house, and you have mold, no matter what, I'm going to advise that it's best to do absolutely everything. Otherwise, I could be held liable.

Even if you have me out and tell me, "I want a new crawl space door," I'd have to be honest and point out anything that you might have going on, "That's fine. We can do just a door," I'll tell you, "But what you should really do is spend $25,000 so your house doesn't fall apart someday."

"It looks like it's about to fall apart?" you'll ask.

"No," I'll say. "But it will. They always do. Eventually."

"When?"

"When they do."

"Why?"

"Law of averages. When you look at enough crawl spaces, you can only assume that each one trends toward shit show."

The world is full of imaginative people who want the best for themselves as compensation for the least possible investment, so you have to walk into every interaction with a suspicion that you might get outplayed.

As far as I know, any area with dead organic material and a consistent relative humidity above 60% grows mold eventually.

To read relative humidity, I use a hygrometer, but I can't tell what brand my current hygrometer is. I have worn it smooth with dirty fingers, and all the painted words have fallen away. I have used other hygrometers. I don't know which one is best. A hygrometer tells you the level of humidity in the crawl.

The best place to get a read is where the joists meet the subfloor. You get your meter right near the home's carpentry package. Heat and vapor rise. Your whole house is made to vent heat at the roof and suck cool air in through vents in your foundation. It's called the stack effect. Which is a fun word to say: Stack, stack, stack.

4. Moisture

I have two moisture meters. One is a pin moisture reader that I use on wood, and one is a pinless moisture reader that

I use on block. Except, my pinless moisture reader is broken, and I never used it much anyway. If a block is wet, you can tell.

Water leaves a mark. Blocks that used to be wet look sweat-stained. The sweat staining is called phosphorescence. Its minerals removed from the block when water makes its way through. The thing about blocks is, they're usually hollow. The thing about hollow things is, they can fill up with water. The foundation wall of your home can get waterlogged so bad that the wooden carpentry package of your floor soaks up the water and begins to rot.

Wet wood is different. Wet wood can kind of look dry. Any wood with a moisture level higher than 16% begins to actively rot. Wet wood bends. Wet wood compresses. It can be impossible to correct.

Think about the legs of a rocking chair. They used to be straight. To bend them, they soaked them. They got the wood waterlogged and applied pressure.

If you took a dry rocking chair leg and tried to straighten it, it'd crack in half.

Wood under a house can get saturated by humidity. I've seen subfloors condensate so bad, the joists basically rained.

The best place to get a read on wood moisture is the lowest part of the wood. Humidity rises. Condensation falls. I mean, under your house is a whole other atmosphere.

5. Level

People who have never done manual labor or construction are delusional about what is achievable. They mix up thoughts and actions. They think thinking a thing through—and having a thing make sense in your mind—means that you can translate that sense into reality. You absolutely cannot.

There is theory. There is practice.

You can know what you're doing and not be able to do what you know. It's like when you give away the joke at the wrong time in the punchline. The ideas are there, but what is it?

"I put a level on my floor," a customer once told me. "The

floor slopes like a dadgum ramp. It drops like a quarter of an inch."

"Drops a quarter of an inch from what?"

"From here to here."

"Yeah, but from when to when?"

"No. It's a distance. You don't get it. From here," the customer pointed at one part of his floor, "to here," the customer pointed to another part.

"Yeah, but were you here when they built it?"

"The house is a 100 years old. I'm 37."

"A lot of things built 100 years ago weren't even level 100 years ago."

"It hasn't always been this way though."

"Are you sure?

"Positive."

"And how long have you lived here?"

"Seven months."

A laser level is the best way to determine if a surface has moved, but it can give you false positives because craftsmen, as good as they might be, do not have laser precision execution. They are human. There is variance.

Mostly, you can assume that anything over a 1/4" difference was an accident or wasn't original to the home, but with older homes, who knows? Houses built in the 1800s were made from timbers often hewed by hand.

The best laser I ever owned was a Hilti Green Dot self-leveling laser. It looked like a robot head and you placed it on a tripod, and it either spun a laser line in a 360, or you could hold a steady dot. The beam that resulted from the 360 spin was a solid green line that looked like this:

This you use to see what might be out of place, and what might have moved.

Pretend this sentence is a joist.

The base of every letter is the same distance from the line below, and thus the sentence is level, hasn't moved. Sits how it would naturally be installed.

This sentence   much.

           not so

The laser shows you where things used to be, and I guess there's a little mystery in the laser light. When you're down there in the dark and the dust is swirling and the laser is painting it green with light.

6. Drawn & Quoted

I am currently using an iPad to produce all my proposals, drawings, and designs. I use an app called ArcSite, which is basically a computer-assisted drawing tool that helps you simplify job designs.

I'm a big fan. I draw each home and create each job. I discuss these proposals as I'm at each customers' house, and it's easy because I have my diagram and my pictures and my photos of jobs we've installed and PDF's of home construction and PDF's of home foundation case studies. Selling is a little bit harder than estimating, but a good estimate and proposal helps you sell.

The first time I ever drew a house, I drew it for an engineer. I used graph paper and a pencil. iPads weren't even a thing. In 20 years, crawl spaces will probably draw themselves.

But for all the tools, there are only a few things you can do to fix a foundation.

You can drain it with a sump pump and buried perforated drainpipe. You can encapsulate it with thick plastic. You can lift it with piers. You can support it with jacks. You can switch out the wood. You can brace the walls with either anchors or beams. You can add a dehumidifier that dries and purifies air.

There seem to be infinite kinds of customers, but there are patterns of behavior.

You could probably collect data on everyone I talk to and make some kind of chart—these types of people buy these types of things. Consistently, the strangest customers are the ones who have no intention of fixing their house.

A few weeks ago, I went to see a woman who had been divorced seven times. She had been pretty. She hadn't aged well. Fallen halo effect.

She was selling her home, and she wanted to make sure she'd pass inspection.

Right before I got in her crawl she said:

"I have a black snake down there, but he's the sweetest. All he does is come out and kill my mice. He won't bother you I don't think."

"In the crawl? A pet snake?"

"No. No. Not a pet. I mean, he's just part of the house. He's friendly."

"Have you visited the snake? In its crawl? They're different when they're defensive. If it touches me, I'll probably kill it." I had both feet through the crawl door, and I was just about to slide down into the muck. My headlamp was on already, and when I looked up to speak to the homeowner, she shielded her eyes. I turned it off.

"It's just a black snake," she said. "I call it Samson."

"Why?"

"He doesn't have hair."

"I can't promise anything."

She was looking off at nothing, presumably thinking about her snake. "I guess go ahead," she said. You could sense her disapproval. "I'm not buying anything if I don't need it though."

"Snakes don't live in clean crawls," I told her.

I turned my headlamp back on.

She covered her eyes with her hand.

"Wish Samson luck," I said and slid out of her view.

Her crawl wasn't terrible. I didn't see her snake. I didn't sell her a single solution. For all I know, Samson is slithering down there right now, only a whole different family lives there, and Samson doesn't even have a name anymore.

YOUNGEST DAUGHTER CAMEO #1

My youngest daughter has a freckle right between her eyes, and I try to send her messages through it because once I got too high on an airplane and I was certain the plane was about to fall from the sky. There was heavy turbulence, and a suspicious man in an N95 kept getting up and changing seats, and a stewardess ran toward the cockpit, and a great orange light filled up one side of our plane, and the passengers all started praying. I touched my fingertips together and I whispered inside my mind at her freckle so that she knew I was dying but that I would always love her and she could always talk to me just like this—through her freckle. It sits perfectly right between her eyes: it's so symmetrical, you can surely talk to it. We call it her third eye. Or her freckle-ogical. And we were sitting at a picnic table that overlooked the cemetery, because she is five years younger than her older sister, and she doesn't like walking that far, yet.

We were practicing. I was sending her words through her freckle one at a time.

"I'm sending it," I told her.

We sat quietly a good while, and I held my fingertips together and she put a fingertip on her freckle-ogical, and I broadcasted my word, and she tried to receive it, all magically.

"Got it?" I said.

"Got it," she said.

"Okay," I put down my hands. "What is it?"

She pressed her freckle good and hard and lowered her hand. "Cloud," she told me.

"Close," I said. "Internet."

The second time I ever tried to talk to my daughter through her freckle was when I was on that same airplane. It was right after we didn't crash. I closed my eyes. I pressed my fingers together. "Never mind," I told her, once I'd built up the courage to look out the window. "We haven't taken off yet."

My youngest daughter was watching the cemetery. "It's weird how death works," she said. She had a Raina Telgemeier book face down on the park bench beside us. "People get put in the ground and then they get turned back into mud, and then they all come back to life, and that's why there's so many people named Steve."

"It is definitely weird," I said. "Want to try again?"

"Sure," she said. "Go."

I closed my eyes, pressed my fingertips together, and sent a word. "Got it?" I looked at her.

She pressed her freckle and looked deep in my eyes and nodded hard. "Rabbit," she said.

"Ooh, close," I told her. "Wig."

CRAWL SPACE TEXT THREAD #2

Germ: I sold 10K in anchors, motherfuckers LFG. How do they work?

> **Darby:** What?

> > **Cowboy Dan:** Germ probably sold them boat anchors.

> **Darby:** You don't know how they work?

Germ: Hit goal already this month, and we still got nearly two weeks left.

> **Darby:** What was wrong with the house?

Germ: It was a basement. Cowboy Dan said that all basements need anchors.

> > **Cowboy Dan:** Eventually, dipshit.

> **Darby:** Why did they have us out?

Germ: Water in the basement.

> > **Cowboy Dan:** The way all babies will eventually need urns and caskets.

> **Darby:** Did you sell them drainage?

> > **Cowboy Dan:** But I guess everything's always cheaper today than tomorrow.

> **Darby:** Anchors hold up the walls. Were the walls failing? Were there cracks?

Cowboy Dan: Because the cost of labor should always go up.

Germ: I don't think there were cracks.

Cowboy Dan: There will be now.

Darby: Do they think their basement will be dry now? You know it won't be dry.

Cowboy Dan: Well, holes.

Darby: Dan, shut the fuck up. You can talk on Monday when you tell us how you got to be so fucking old.

Cowboy Dan: I'm a top guy. Teasing Germ is Top Guy things.

Germ: Did I mess up?

Kepler: You'll never have to go to Ohio.

Darby: Probably.

Kepler: Not for work anyhow.

Cowboy Dan: Why would anyone go to Ohio for anything other than work?

Germ: So not all basements need them??

Cowboy Dan: Eventually. Eventually.

Germ: . . .

Darby: . . .

Kelper: . . .

Cowboy Dan: Eventually.

7

Germ doesn't know much, but he was right when he said Delta 8 is legal in Indiana, and I got so high I emailed Carlo Rovelli.

Delta 8 is a kind of loophole byproduct that emerged from our cannabis laws. It's kind of a problem in search of an answer. People weren't begging to have fake weed available at gas stations. There is legal hemp that cannot get you high without chemistry. Hemp that needs chemistry to get you high is called Delta 8. They take legal hemp and extract the cannabinoids and boil them down and it's legal because it's not illegal, and they sell that at gas stations cooked into gummy bears because it's an unjust society and people like to make money and get high.

My daughter says, "What is this book even about?" She picks up a Rovelli book I have by my bed and holds it up at me. "I tried the first few pages and my brain started hurting."

Carlo Rovelli hurts my brain too, but Cowboy Dan got me researching quantum levels and I found some of Rovelli's books after reading Wikipedia. He's a theoretical physicist—a kind of philosopher who looks at quantum theory.

I've read three of his books, but I don't think I can define quantum theory or quantum entanglement—not clearly. I think it's about processes, possibilities, information, connection, and time. And I think that since there are possibilities, and since there is time, there are endless possibilities. We exist "now," and outside of now is infinite. You are a tiny process in a (sea of anything goes / see if anything goes).

From my understanding, "now" is a space—the space in which you can perceive changes instantly. Outside of that space, every single possible thing that could occur is occurring, and until you look, it kind of isn't, but once you look and see, you and that thing are connected forever.

The quantum folks seem extremely impressed by something called the double-slit experiment which shows that atoms both travel as waves and particles depending on whether or not they are watched. Watched, they are particles. Not watched, they are waves. Raindrops or oceans, depending on whether or not you're paying attention, but only once you've paid attention. Who knows what happens if you don't pay attention at all?

Delta 8 is available in lots of Indiana gas stations, but you never know until you go inside—lots of gas stations seem embarrassed by having it, and most of them don't have signs in the front of their stores that say Delta 8. Almost all of them have beer signs.

Asian-owned gas stations and gas stations with no public restrooms will usually have some kind of cannabinoid, but you can't tell that from the parking lot except when you can tell that from the parking lot.

"Funny you should ask that, Imagination Mary Louise Kelly," I'll say and sit in my Prius watching the windows of some gas station in some town. "It's hard to say what makes a gas station look like it sells Delta 8, but I would definitely say that the more products they sell, the more likely they are to sell something that'll get you high."

I dug up Carlo Rovelli's email address at some Italian University website because I don't think he's so famous that he doesn't check his own email, but it doesn't really matter.

Delta-8 gummies are expensive candy. For $30 you get about 300 milligrams of whatever the Delta 8 active ingredient exactly is—it's supposed to be chemically enhanced legal weed but sometimes it's that and regular weed too by some fortuitous accident—and for most people, 10-50 milligrams is sufficient to get you obliterated for at least half of the daytime even if you eat it for breakfast.

I had eaten 300 mgs in one go and dipped into some Carlo Rovelli book—*The Order of Time* or *Helgoland*—and I had forgotten I was stupid, and I had pretended to contemplate math.

I became goofy about existence. I had looked for ghosts in the laser that day in the crawls. Sitting in pitch black listening to the laser calibrate in the mold-heavy air. It's self-leveling, the laser: it has to show an even, infinite line. If it's out of level—

and it will spin itself cattywampus—the light turns off until the system reconfigures. Cowboy Dan is probably full of shit, but there are plenty of liars I believe lies from, plenty of liars I'll sit in the dark for.

I wasted hours in the muck with my headlamp off watching my Hilti strobe its arcade-colored magic, nervous in the darkness hoping to see dead faces lurch at me through the air.

I wanted a childhood feeling—to feel afraid. To see ancient crawl peoples revealed by my Hilti.

When I was in fifth grade, my friends and I turned off the lights in the elementary school bathroom and whispered at the mirrors and pretended to see red eyes come alive. Bloody Mary. Bloody Mary.

And I wanted it to feel like between the second and third time you said her name, with the spiders scurrying all around me and the snakes licking the air.

I sat cross-legged in a sheet of light trying to allow a moment to happen, something consequential and dark, but my laser just strummed dust and warbled out against walls, and I saw nothing but waves and particles depending where I was looking.

So, my email to Carlo Rovelli went like this:

Dear Carlo,

> I have a question. I work in crawl spaces. I inspect them, and I have read every book of yours I can find translated into English.

> I currently use a Hilti Green Dot Self-Leveling Laser. Do you know the brand? Do you have crawl spaces in Italy?

> I was down in a crawl, and I had set up my laser to see if a foundation was level,

because when you're under a home, you can run a laser line down the mortar between the foundation-wall blocks and see if a house is sinking in spots. You can also run a laser line down a main beam to see if it is beginning to bow. Same with joist bottoms, but that's not really the point here.

The point here is this: my laser was spinning green light, and my headlamp was off, and I looked back toward the laser, and it was like I was in a different dimension, because there was a plane of green light that dust motes danced in, only I know the dust motes weren't dancing at all. They were just being motes and the air was just air.

So, I guess what I'm asking is this: if I wasn't looking at it, would all that dust be in different locations? Or does that only work with particles even smaller than that? Also, can old information hang around in there? In the crawl spaces?

Like, my laser has one job: to show me where things used to be. But can it maybe show me other old information? I know a guy who says a laser can show you ghosts, but I've only ever seen dust. But if you have to look at something to see it, can you look things into place? Like, can your awareness of information change the information before you've even been informed by it?

*Also, do you have Delta 8 in Italy or do
you just drink wine? If they don't have
Delta 8, and you'd like, I could mail you
some. Also, if you're ever in Indiana and
want to look at a laser with me in a crawl
space, just let me know.*

All best,
Cook

My wife said, "Are you emailing Carlo Rovelli?"

Who knows how long she'd been watching. She stood there, and the living room was around me, but I had entered another dimension with Carlo Rovelli that we could only access through my computer screen.

"It's porn," I said and minimized a few windows.

"It's not either," she said. "You're whispering and typing. You don't whisper-type at porn."

"Maybe I'm commenting."

"If you're commenting on porn," my wife said, "we're getting divorced. What kind of monster does that? What could even be said?" She walked over and closed my laptop. "Take the oldest," she told me. "On a walk," she said. "Come back when you're less high."

"Fine," I said, because I had my phone on me just in case Rovelli emailed back and I hoped that a walk would waste enough time for him to compose a return email, so I shouted, "Kid." And I shouted, "Come on." And I nearly screamed, "Mom says we're going for a walk."

NOW & MAYBE

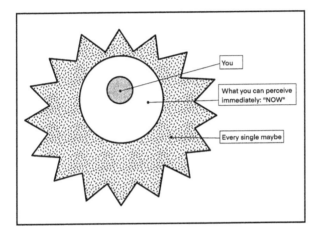

8

We headed for the cemetery, and I kept checking my phone for a reply from Rovelli. I felt like a cloud salesman at a Delta 8 amusement park. High. Silly. Nearly unable to think. The air seemed the color of the concrete streets. The grass felt like playdough. I focused on nothing. My eyes were open, and the world looked gone to me.

"Do you think I could change a crawl space with my mind?" I asked my daughter as we plodded. You could hear our steps, occasionally a car coughed down the road.

My daughter said, "Change it to what? A rainbow? A screwdriver?"

"No. Not into something absurd. Just something it could be. Supposedly anything that can actually happen, so long as you can't perceive it, is actually happening."

"What?"

"I don't know. It has to do with how particles travel or land. I think it means I should be able to choose. Like with my mind. Like before I open a crawl door, I can change it. Just choose to open the door onto a bad foundation. Or forget it even being a crawlspace. Can you change things with your mind?"

My daughter seemed to thin her eyes at a thing that wasn't there, concentrating on a thought as though she could see it. "Like manifesting?" she said. "Isn't that like the law of attraction?"

"No. It's quantum physics, and I don't mean eventually. More like *shazam*."

"Like *shazam*: a worse crawl space?"

"Or *shazam*: whatever."

"I doubt it. You might be able to manifest something, but I don't think you do it with your brain. I'm currently manifesting becoming a nepo baby. It takes a lot of vibes. It's like your curse."

"I'm not cursed."

"Do you even hear yourself?" My daughter looked at me like I never learned to read. "Your energy is distorted. Do you think it'll rain?"

I honestly didn't understand how it wasn't raining. It looked like if you squeezed the air hard enough, it would drip. "Maybe. Mom had me bring an umbrella." I pulled it from my back pocket, and instantly it started to lightly sprinkle.

"See, mom has good energy," my daughter held her palm to the sky. "She manifested rain."

I took my phone from my pocket. No notifications. "I want to manifest something," I said.

I put away my phone, opened the umbrella, and my oldest daughter leaned against me and we moved toward the cemetery, across the street, through the gravestones, huddled together beneath our black umbrella, watching the light rain drizzle from the umbrella's ribs.

"Let's go back to that grave with no name," I said. "I want to look at it better. See if we can maybe figure out the name through the scratches."

"Or," she said, "even better. We can vibe a name onto it."

"Vibe what?"

"I mean, if all the names are out there happening," her head hit my umbrella hand and the umbrella shed droplets, "shouldn't we be able to pick one for it? Let's try Harvey."

"When you say it like that, it seems stupid."

"Dis—tort—ed," my daughter said. "Give me one reason we shouldn't at least try."

I couldn't. I thought a little too long. "You're distorted."

"He retorted," my daughter said.

"Shut up."

"Bad energy."

"Fine," I said, "Harvey, Harvey, Harvey!" and we wandered in the direction of the nameless grave that Harvey found mesmerizing, both of us trying to carve his name into a headstone with our vibes.

I understood Harvey's obsession. It's better to spend your life enamored. It's why the internet is so addictive. You learn about something, and need to learn something else. That's nature. Answers make questions. Thirteen point eight billion years ago, space became aware of time, and because of that, the universe created itself—a giant encounter between two unfathomable things.

"We vibed it wrong," my daughter said.

I was looking at my phone and walking along letting my daughter guide us between tombstones, checking to see if I had any emails. "You can't read it from that far away."

"No, but look." She pointed ahead of us, her hand out in the rain. "We put him there."

Up ahead, beside the nameless grave, Harvey stood with his hand on the presumably defaced tombstone, a dopey silhouette in a sea of gray, contemplating a rock that meant nothing to anyone.

I had zero notifications. "What a waste of vibes," I said, and my daughter yelled, "Harvey!"

He turned to us and stood still and calm, watching us move toward him with examining eyes. When we got to him, his cheeks were wet and red. He stood feebly in the grass. "Bullshit," he said. "I was just thinking about y'all. It's like I brought you here with my mind. I figured out whose grave it is."

"Did you ask around?" my daughter said.

"Offer them a little more than a twenty?"

"Didn't need to," said Harvey. "I decided there's not a body here at all. It's probably some kind of sick fucking joke." He clenched his teeth. "Went to a doctor about that. The cussing." He closed his eyes and smiled. "He says it's nothing physical. Probably repressed resentments coming out as bad words." He opened his eyes again. "I'd rather have a tumor."

"See," my oldest daughter told me. "That's basically distorted energy leading to distorted outcomes. It's basically a doctor saying he's cursed."

"Is that what he's saying?"

"He also said my posture was getting worse, and I should use my walker less, but I don't really care about posture. Sometimes I think I wouldn't mind falling though. But just one last time. And for forever."

"You don't think you'll figure it out?" my daughter asked. "The resentment?"

"Of course not. I can barely remember anything. I'd have to retrace my steps. Maybe it's with my hat." He wiped rain off his bald head.

"Did you lose it?" my daughter said. "I can crochet you one. I have lots of gray yarn."

"I don't really think it's with my hat."

"Or you could wait until I get more yarn."

"Gray's fine," Harvey said. Then, turning to me, "You go all over Indiana, right? Looking at houses?"

"Pretty much," I said. "Not many places I don't get."

Harvey gave his wet head one last wipe and flung droplets from his fingers. "I need to go to Terre Haute. Ever get out that way?"

"On occasion."

"Think if I wanted to retrace a few steps, you might be able to give me a ride?"

My phone chimed in my pocket. "A ride?" I said. I was planning on blaming work. Telling Harvey that it'd be a professional liability to have passengers, but I took my phone from my pocket to check the notification. "I'm not sure I'm allowed," I said, and I looked at my phone, and it was a reply from Carlo Rovelli.

"Is that the guy from the book?" my daughter said, because she was so close to me she could see the screen of my phone, but I lifted the phone closer to my face, out of her view, and opened the email. It said this:

> This is an automatic response. I am overwhelmed by the number of mails I receive. Many of these are wonderful and extremely kind, and I would very much like to answer everybody, but there is no human way I could do so. My very sincere apologies.

Also, at present I do not accept any
invitation to conferences or talks.
Thanks anyway.

Carlo

"Why wouldn't you be able to take him?" my daughter
asked. "It'd probably help your energy."

Harvey returned to looking at the nameless grave, mumbled
something to himself that I couldn't quite hear but that I figured
was cussing.

And I looked back at the email. Read the part again where
he said, "there is no human way I could."

"I mean, I don't want you to break any rules," Harvey said,
still contemplating the scratched-away name.

"He might," my oldest daughter said. "He breaks the rules
all the time."

"It was an automatic response," I said. *But could my energy
have changed that?*

"What's that mean?" said my daughter.

I looked at my daughter. I looked at Harvey. I looked at the
grave. "Probably pretty soon." I looked back at the email. "I'm
all over everywhere."

A long silence passed, and the email said the same thing
over and over again as I read it.

"I could pay gas," said Harvey. "Or buy you a beer."

"He doesn't drink," my daughter said.

"Even better," said Harvey. "I won't have to worry about us
getting pulled over."

I closed the email, opened the email again, but all the
words were the same.

I closed the email, looked at Harvey. "Okay," I told him. I
opened the email again, but it hadn't changed.

"You will?" my daughter said. "For the good energy?

"Yes," I said again, and again I closed and opened the
email. Closed an opened it. "I'll give you a ride to Terre Haute,"
I said so the universe could hear me.

"This is amazing," my daughter said. "I know it will work. And I'll get to work on the hat."

"I'll be indebted forever," Harvey said, and then he wrote down his phone number for me on a piece of paper, and we planned on me calling when I knew something, and my daughter talked a bit more about yarn, and the whole walk home from the cemetery I tried to change Carlo's message with my vibes.

This is ~~an~~ automatic ~~response~~. I am overwhelmed ~~by the number of mails I receive~~. ~~Many of these are~~ wonderful and extreme~~ly kind~~, and I would very much like to answer ~~everybody, but there is no human way I could do so. My very sincere apologies.~~

~~Also, at present~~ I ~~do not~~ accept any invitation to conferences or talks. Thanks ~~anyway.~~

Carlo

9

It was the last Monday of the month, and Cowboy Dan stood at the podium, staring into the audience of inspectors, his eyes tucked under the brim of his leather cowboy hat, perplexingly.

"Where's Darby?" said Germ, and Cowboy Dan looked down at the podium, in deep focus.

"Did he get a DUI?" Kipler said. "On the way in? Was he drinking already?"

"Probably never stopped," said Germ.

No one laughed. The words hovered casually. Men aren't supposed to drink before breakfast, but some occupations are entangled with antiquity. Long ago, a bearded man in a cabin at dawn chugged a flagon of barley wine, loaded his rifle, and walked into the woods, and from that moment until our Monday morning meeting—if you only knew how to look for it—a dotted line connected us. "It's the last Monday of the month," I said. "Employee Presentations. Cowboy Dan. We drew straws."

"Holy shit," said Kipler. "That's today? And no one brought snacks? No one reminded us? Coffee? Donuts? Triangle sandwiches with all the crusts cut off? Me, I like the crust. Some people think that's where the vitamins are, but they're just getting bread confused with a potato. Lots of vitamins in the skin of the potato. But bread crust isn't a potato skin."

Darby stuck his head in the salesroom door. "Christ, Kipler. What the fuck are you talking about?"

"People get vitamins in the bread crust wrong."

"I'm not even sure what language that is. There were three emails last week and it's in a text thread. You could've brought the sandwiches. You could've cut the crusts."

Kipler picked up his phone. Thumbed some things. Scrolled. "No shit," he said. "My bad." And he set his phone down like it all hadn't happened.

Darby dangled half in the salesroom, half in the hall. "I'll call a few of you out for conferences. Otherwise, pay attention to Dan. He's a silver alert waiting to happen, but he sells more than most. Rumor is, he's 200 years old."

Cowboy Dan was at his most comfortable in mud, but someone was making him stand behind a podium. It felt like a city council meeting or court. One of the slogans that hung on the wall read: *It has to get done to be done.*

Darby said, "Cowboy Dan, floor's yours. Germ, we're starting with you. Conference. Hallway. Right now. Go!"

Germ stood up and loped toward the door, his beefy shoulders up and down in animal fashion. "Embrace that pain," he said—wild and in tune with the KoolAid of crawl space and capitalism. He clapped twice and heaved aloft on tiptoes the way a cartoon wrestler in a leotard might. Twinkle. Dinkle. Dink. Disappeared down the hallway with Darby, and pulled the door closed behind them. We remaining inspectors sat watching Cowboy Dan.

He looked befuddled. He fidgeted paper. Tapped fingers on the podium. Hung his head so the brim of his hat hid his eyes. The salesroom felt bewitched with him at the front of it. A shiver crossed us all. Unease. Full-bodied silence. The passage of time. I began to feel nervous for Dan. Did he know he wasn't talking? Was he giving his speech in his head?

The moments felt measured incorrectly. If only there existed some tool that read relative awkwardness like relative humidity, and some machine to extract that awkward energy from the air as though it were water and piss it out to be pumped away. A kind of de-awkwarder.

"I don't have formal education beyond Sunday school and Sunday sermons," said Cowboy Dan, his voice dusty from decades of crawl exposure—weathered and moldy. "But I'm old enough that my words make me sound smart. And before I am done," Dan checked some notes, "here today," he moved something, "you will know both how I came to this profession and the deeper magic of your lasers."

Kipler cleared his throat. "Deeper magic of our lasers?"

Cowboy Dan ignored him and scanned the room. "If you pay attention, riddles solve themselves, but it's not the universe's job to answer our questions before we even think to ask them. Conundrums predate clarity."

He turned a sheet of paper. "I started doing this the same way we all started doing this. I needed a job. Most of my people were workers. My uncles were mechanics, and my aunts cleaned houses. My father worked railroad. But my mother studied flowers.

"He was a conductor, my father. It was his job to make sure the train left the station on time. He liked the passengers. He marveled at the clock. He knew humans were mostly water. And he was mystified that a timepiece could synchronize them all and put them on a track to become a machine filled with that water, a sort of river of people in harmony with time and industry. A kind of wave. Heading in the same direction."

I looked around to see who was paying attention, and everyone else was looking around to see who was paying attention.

"My mother, on the other hand," Cowboy Dan continued, "studied the desiccation of flowers. Clocking how long it took a flower's pedals to parch after picking them. And they would talk about time and water and people, and I wanted to be a ship captain for some reason—the way a child's mind will gather evidence and come to verdicts that don't quite tally. And I began to read about oceans.

"Every ocean touches every ocean, and every drop of every river will one day be taken to the sky and redeposited as rain, and once a drop of water becomes rain enough times, it is bound to be ocean bound, and thus every drop of water on Earth will someday be part of the same body of water, if even just momentarily. Not every drop touches every drop, but every drop has touched a drop that has touched a drop that has touched a drop. Bodies of water moving into bodies of water. And we are water, included in each of those waves." Cowboy Dan nodded out at us as though he'd predetermined to pause at this point in the speech. And then, "When I moved out on my own, I took a job on the Florida coast in a boat captained by a one-armed Mexican who the crew called

Señor Starboard, on account of his right arm being the one missing, the way you might call a one-armed man Lefty so long as it was his left arm that was gone. But while I found my accommodations and duties fitting for my demeanor and predispositions—squabbing the poop deck, mending nets, feeding the parrots—I was not suited to the ocean going part of ocean going. It sickened me."

"Wait," said Kipler. "Cowboy Dan, were you a pirate?"

He stood silent a moment. "Nearly," he said.

"Then why do we all call you Cowboy Dan?"

"Because of my hat," Cowboy Dan said. "I've worked with cows even less than on boats. See, we hadn't cleared the harbor when, upon feeling the ship heave, I saw instantly that I could not be in that vast, moving, and endless creation. It made me sick to pitch and wobble, and, saying as much to Señor Starboard, I was made to walk the plank in semi-jest, my captain electing to have me leap into the water and swim ashore rather than head back to dock." Cowboy Dan lifted his hat and adjusted its position. "It was fine. I didn't want to waste their time, and I had no possessions other than the clothes on my back, and it was sort of amusing stepping out on the plank above the water, Señor Starboard close behind me with a drawn dagger at my back."

"What if we bought you a bandana?" Kipler said.

"At the plank's end I turned to face my captain. I wanted to see his eyes, but as soon as our eyes locked, I felt the heavy urge to vomit, and, being a ship captain and presumably having seen the pre-demeanor of countless seasick voyagers, Señor Starboard pressed a palm to my chest and drove me back away from the ship, sending me off the plank, and I dropped like a stone, plunged into the saltwater, watched the ocean engulf me, watched as my lost breath bubbled away, and when I emerged from the surface, and gulped for air, I could hear the crew rejoicing, their laughter and banter fading as the ship sailed off to be lost forever from my sight on the horizon.

"I turned and paddled toward the shore, swimming as a

sad dog might, but, hoisting my body onto the sand, I saw, extending from a bluff, a drainage pipe that water dribbled from, and this dribbling landed in the ocean water, and it occurred to me that while you could trace every drop of water to the ocean, you could also trace that same water in reverse. The drainage pipe was, in some haphazard and paltry way, filling the seas, and I decided right then and there on that beach to chase the water back through its endless journey to its source, and in doing so, I would trace the journey of all things living on this blue planet in this vast universe, in this infinite reality of existence, in this chaos, and in this order. The source. The start. When you are confused, you start there."

Cowboy Dan reached under the podium, lifted a bottle of water, and took a long drink. He swallowed hard. Wiped his mouth with the back of a hand, set down the water bottle, and continued. "Luckily for me," he said, "the drainage pipe was 4' in diameter, and I thought: Now. Now is always as good a time as any, and I climbed into the drainage pipe. And I pulled myself toward the source of the water, leaving behind the light of day, and leaving behind my dreams of being a boat captain and moving toward my career as a crawl space man. A career of now. A life of moving things back to the start."

The door flung open, and Germ sauntered in with a goofy face on his goofy fucking face saying, "Top guy things!" And shucked himself into his seat like we were all fighter pilots but it was a movie about him.

"Cook," said Darby. "Your turn."

"Do I have to?" I said. "I'm enjoying the story."

"Mandatory," said Darby. "Especially with your numbers."

I nodded at Darby, winked at Cowboy Dan for moral support, got up glumly and followed Darby to the hall.

Once we left the meeting room, Darby lowered his tone. "I bet that old goat will talk for a few hours. Want breakfast?"

"I mean," I said, "how long is the presentation supposed to last? I wanted to see the next part. The thing about lasers."

"No set limits on presentations. The meeting can go until noon." Darby had a faraway look about him. He was there and somewhere else.

"It's 7:30."

"Yeah, but I think he'll still be going when we get back."

"Should I grab my stuff? Like my satchel?"

"If you need it, but I'll buy breakfast."

"But we're coming back?" I was thinking lasers. I was thinking ghosts.

"Yeah, yeah," said Darby. "I mean, we have to."

As we walked away, I could hear Cowboy Dan talking inside, and I was happy because Cowboy Dan was still just talking about water.

DeAwkwarder by *Trap*

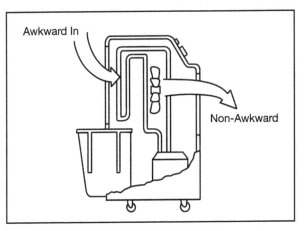

It clears the weird so you can vibe good.

10

I have deep sympathy for all addicts, having myself gone through throes. My worst days were in South Texas before I moved to Indiana, drinking and popping pills when my daughters were still young. I drank so much that when I was sober I'd have anxiety attacks, fidget, my heart racing and out of sync with my eyes—my baseline 'wasted'. I found a doctor to prescribe me Klonopin. I'd dissolve two on my tongue, get a plastic bottle of Mescal, and drive along the border wall watching for drones and crossers, spooked every time I ever saw either. Bodies in the distance moving crouched through the thickets—black, flying robots zipping around until they hovered still.

I'd get hammered and buy a few gallons of water and set them along the highway for crossers. Water destroys a home but saves a household. The crossers were drenched from the river and thirsty.

I'd walk a bridge over the Rio Grande into Mexican border towns where I could get anything. On the way over, beggars with children called out for money from the riverbank. Just beyond that: Codeine syrup, Xanax, Cocaine. Prescription drugs auctioned off by something like carnival barkers who stood in front of pharmacies that also sold pets. Cocaine you'd buy off whichever local had the biggest belt buckle on Benito Juarez Ave. A pound of dirt weed was $35. I've never liked needles, but I'll smoke or swallow most anything when I'm on a bender. Get it upside down on occasion: Snorting drugs made to swallow and swallowing drugs made to smoke.

You'd get half bogged out your mind before crossing the Rio Bravo—daytime, Ernest Hemingway, white-privilege drinking—the river called something else, just the same water from another side. There was a bar called Belly to Belly, and they had a mechanical bull with customized settings, and every time I crossed I had them put it to "Pony Boy" and tried to ride it to heaven.

I'd drink all day with my poet friends in the hallucinatory

South Texas light: it's brighter than anywhere else I've ever been—the shadows, darker. Every surface of every building was painted like an Easter egg. I stayed in a perpetual state of "just learning Spanish" because that's the best type of Spanish a white boy can know. Mariachis wandered in and out playing corridos. A kind of waltz with three chords about heroes who killed white people.

Pound tequila and rattle around under the high sun aimless. Get home and get in my own head. Hike along irrigation canals, throwing rocks at the nutria and turtles. When the moon came up: scream at it.

I probably looked homeless.

My oldest daughter turned five and started to know. Her eyes landed on me different. She'd make me pinky promise not to drink every time I left the house. She had a necklace with a little pouch on it, and she'd pretend it was filled with magic dust.

"I'm going to throw this on you."

"What is it?"

"Magic dust."

"What's it do?"

"Keeps you from drinking."

The dust didn't work, but I couldn't stand telling my daughter she wasn't magical.

I found an AA group that met at 7:30 every morning, and two old men— Ramón and Max—talked me through a kick.

"All you have is the present," Ramón said, "everything else is cucuys."

"Absolute surrender," said Max. "Exist in the sunshine of the spirit."

I knew a guy back then who had famously bottomed out and used other people's money to smoke $70k in crack. I'd fall off the wagon and email him bullshit. He told me to get tattoos to remind me not to fuck up. I did. They were my first tattoos, and they didn't work. But I guess they're still on me, so maybe they're working now.

I can't decide what I think of using Delta 8. I'm not

technically sober. I just don't drink.

Darby, on the other hand, is an absolute alcoholic, but he's high functioning. He could drink all day and not miss a deadline. I never saw him stumble, but if you weren't used to what it was he was, you might have worried over him. Some people just stay pickles and it's all okay. Like Christopher Hitchens or Winston Churchill.

So, when we got in his truck, it was clean. But there was that distant smell of alcoholism—the only addiction that reminds me of Christians. Sour and yeasty. The stench of old reverends.

"Want a beer?" Darby said.

"It's 7:35."

"Stop. I feel judged."

"Usually when I have breakfast beer I'm going through shit."

Darby opened the center console of his truck and tugged out a blue Solo cup and reached under his chair and fished out a Busch Light tallboy. He poured half the beer into the cup, put the half can of beer in the cup holder of his car door, and we drove away with his foamy beer jostling in his hand. "Nah. I mean, the girl is on my case forever, but it's like it doesn't even make sense. I act exactly how I've always acted. I work the same amount. I drink the same amount. She met me, saw how I lived, wanted to move in with me, and then wanted me to change everything. I've never dated a girl with a job more adult than mine. Marcy does retail. Like, do people even do that anymore? When's the last time you went to a store to buy clothes that wasn't Costco?"

"Where we going?"

"To get more beer." Darby smiled at me. I mean, he took his eyes off the road, looked at me, and smiled. One hand on the wheel. One hand holding an alcoholic beverage. The road racing beneath us. The sun barely up. Laws being broken. Other drivers endangered. Me in my seatbelt, and Darby just smiling. "I don't ever text and drive," he said. "And that's just as bad, and every time I ever pass anyone on the highway, they're looking at their phones. What's that called?" Darby sipped his beer then looked back at the road.

"Distracted driving?"

"No. When you kind of compare the two? Like, because I hate people who text and drive. They should all go to jail."

"Two wrongs make a right?"

"I think it's more complicated than that."

"Moral relativism?"

"That definitely sounds better."

We pulled up to a gas station and Darby slid his truck into park. "Need anything?"

"I had some Delta-8 in my bag. I would've grabbed it."

He picked up his phone, looked at it, and his face went weird. Angry. Tense. "That weed shit?" He thumb-bashed a reply.

"It's Delta-8," I said. "If they sell it, I'll take it. They don't always. I'm just like you. I like feeling different than this."

"Fair," Darby said. He put his phone in his console. "This girl makes me drink." Then he hoofed it into the store.

I took out my phone to waste time, opened my email and thought. Different response, different response, different response from Carlo Rovelli. But when I clicked on his email it was still the same old thing, and I said, "What do you think, Imagination Mary Louise Kelly? Think they'll have Delta-8? Or will I once again be cursed?"

I have a memo in my phone called "Things Recently Blamed on JP" and typed, "No D8 with Da" because my energy was so bad there was no way I was getting what I wanted, but then Darby moseyed out with a few more 24 oz. cans of beer and a pouch of edibles, carrying all of it like it was something you should always buy before 8:00 AM, and I put my phone away and didn't finish the note.

Darby opened the truck cabin and tossed the edibles at me. "If all candy was that expensive, there wouldn't be any fat kids. Does it work?"

I looked at the pouch, opened it up, ate a few candies. "It better." I chewed and chewed. "It's an unregulated industry though. Might be potent. Might be bleach."

"Let's do stoner music," Darby said. "For the drive." He fired up the truck and diddled his phone. "Floyd," he said. He chucked the truck in reverse, and messed with A/C vents, and synthesizers droned in like golden lasers through the speakers, and Darby took a big pull of his beer, and hooted, "Shine on. Shine on. Shine on," and I felt sad for him, the same way I feel sad for all people who don't listen to new music after high school.

We sped out through the Indiana countryside, aimlessly. The sky felt eternal. The morning, golden. Milky fog filled the ditches, poured over the road in thin fingers. The deep green of young soybean and corn stalks. The high, heavy yellow of hay. All the land in parcels, every parcel the color of some crop. A black asphalt highway cut through it all. The music swept across the glades, hung the way the day hung, like damp sheets on clotheslines, and I zoned off and considered everything that was green. Green because of water.

I'd been to homes that back up to corn fields, purchased when the corn was high. "When I bought it," the homeowner would say, "the crawl space was dry as a bone. This fall, it flooded."

"Was it right after they harvested?"

Who would know that? That the ground under your house is drier when the cornfield next door is heavy with green crop. Who would consider such a thing?

"How many gallons of water can an acre of corn hold?" I said.

"I'm not a farmer," said Darby. "We might be sending two folks to Ohio." I think he'd been waiting for me to talk. "You *and* Germ." He glugged at his beer, set the Solo cup between his legs, filled it with more beer. "That way he's got someone to check in with. I don't think he understands what he's selling, and he's selling a lot."

"Everything is easy when you do it wrong," I said, "but there's tons of month left."

"There's a week. Your KPI suck ass."

"It doesn't make sense."

Darby took a long drink of beer. "It'll be good."

The music started to underpin all things. The light started to fall in shambles.

"I don't want to," I said. I couldn't elaborate. My tongue and eyebrows felt like clay.

"Of course you don't."

Expensive candy. Old music. A flood of weirdness orchestrated. An undoing of the rational world. The green of the fields. The glow of the day. It all slid askew and Darby's face seemed somehow moored at the center of the discombobulation—bathed in shadows of disorder and persecution.

"I'm not going." I said.

"What time is it?"

"Are you changing the subject?"

"Your numbers are trash."

"I'm not going."

"We'll talk about it back at the office." Darby dialed up the music. David Gilmour sang "Come in here, dear boy."

"I'm not going to Ohio," I hollered over it.

"Bro, you're high as fuck. You've said the same thing three times in a row to me."

The road ran beneath us. I wasn't happy about anything. The synthesizers were synthesizing. The song was about a train, and the train was made of gravy.

11

Of course, most things don't shine, and most trains aren't gravy.

"Do you have a small bladder?" Harvey asked. We'd been driving for less than an hour and were about halfway to Terre Haute where he planned to retrace steps. "My mother had a small bladder. Road trips took forever. She wore diapers toward the end."

I didn't need to piss, and I didn't need a drink. And I didn't even need to stretch my legs. I needed a break from Harvey. When he was standing in the cemetery it must have drained him, and when he was sitting in my car, he had more energy to talk.

I learned he graduated from Trine, "Go Thunder!" how old he was when he lost his virginity, "would you believe eleven years old?" and what he thought about UFOs, "I saw one when I was younger. I was twenty-four or twenty-three. It was stealing energy through a power plant. I was in Colorado. The UFO was sucking electric out through the air, just hovering over the plant. The UFO was swelling and the plant was shrinking, that's how I know that it was sucking energy. Not a ton. Just enough to somehow notice. I threw a stick at it. After a while it flew away."

"I need some candy," I told Harvey when I put my car in park—in a Prius, park is a button.

"Even better," said Harvey. "A sweet tooth."

"Not really," I said. "Different candy."

Harvey followed me in and he headed to the candy section, and I headed to the counter because if they have Delta 8, that's where they keep it. They had a 100MG pack of peach rings, and while I was checking out, Harvey brought a bag of peach rings over from the candy section. "The ones over there are cheaper," he said after hearing the cashier ring me up. "Like, not even half the cost and you get more."

I didn't feel like explaining it to him—that things can look the same and be entirely different things.

We piled back into the car and I drove west out I-70, a soulless stretch of two-lane highway, thick with 18-wheelers taking god knows what to god knows where.

"Can you tell if a house is messed up from the driveway?" Harvey asked. "Like, even before you get out of your car?"

He was looking out the window and we had exited the highway and were working our way through residential streets to his destination, and I had a Delta 8 peach ring glow, and Harvey wanted to listen to jazz so I pulled up some list on Spotify and Cole Porter crooned, "I can hear a lark somewhere begin to sing about it."

"I have to get under them," I said. "To really know what's going on. Why?"

"Nothing," said Harvey. "It's probably fucked."

I was taking Harvey to a home his father built, but I didn't know it then. I wasn't trying to learn anything more about Harvey than he was willing to share, and he was willing to share too much already.

When I pulled him up into the driveway, Harvey sat a moment with his hand on his seatbelt button. "What's your first impression?"

"First impression of what?"

"The house," said Harvey. "Does it look okay? Is it falling apart?"

"I don't know," I said. "It looks like a house, and plenty of houses look good from outside and are rotten beneath. It's like skinny people with bad hearts and fat people who live forever. You can't tell until you can tell."

"Even better," said Harvey. "I guess I'll just figure it out." He undid his seatbelt and opened his door, put a foot down on the pavement and looked back at me. "Wish me luck," he said.

We shook hands and he stepped down from my car and scuffed his way up the driveway, and I put my Prius in reverse and pulled back onto 70 with all the positive energy I could muster pouring off me.

Later that night, once I'd gotten home and was sitting in my living room, my oldest daughter came in. "I forgot to give you

Harvey's hat." She held up a yarn hat that she had crocheted. "I made it and forgot to give it to you."

"The next time I go," I said. "I'll drop it by."

"Did you feel it?" my daughter asked.

"His hat?"

"The energy."

"I have to go to Ohio on Sunday," I told her.

"So?"

"And stay there a week?"

"So?"

"In a hotel with a wrestler bro."

"But did you feel anything change? Like when you dropped Harvey off."

"No," I told her. "Maybe good energy takes a while to get back to you."

"The universe is a process," my daughter told me.

"Well, I wish it would speed up."

Then I got high and Googled "UFO sucking electricity in Colorado," but I didn't find any good articles, so then I just sat cross-legged in the nearly dark, staring at my rug. "I don't even believe in fucking aliens," I said to it.

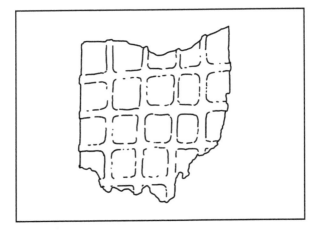

12

"What time did you get here?" Germ asked.

I was in our Ohio hotel, playing pool in the lobby. It was nearly midnight, and I had a 9:00 appointment two hours away. I had the cue in my hand, and I struck a shot, and the four-ball almost went where it was supposed to go, and I told Germ, "A little after nine. Safe enough drive?"

"Safe enough I got here."

"Grab a stick. We can gamble. You'll probably make money." I missed another shot. "You make money at everything else."

"I'm dead and I've never really played pool. Tomorrow though. What time do they do breakfast?"

"Six-thirty. Farm fresh microwaved eggs from a can and waffles. In Texas, at hotels," another miss, "the waffles are shaped like Texas. I don't know what Ohio looks like on a map."

"You could make a waffle shaped like it," said Germ. "But I doubt they do. Guess we'll see at six-thirty."

I played through my game of solo eight ball and watched the late-night hotel people—the workers, the guests—flailing in and out of the lobby like human rags.

Every time I'm in a hotel lobby, I feel like I'm getting the flu. Fluorescent light and hard, flat carpet that's bizarrely patterned. An ice machine hums. The air smells like puddles of indoor-pool water and faint cigarette smoke, and somehow a child's voice is always echoing.

Night arrivals in American hotels are strange creatures. They come in a few forms. They are drunk, or beat, or bereaved. They are either on the road for work, or on the road for vacation, or on the road for a funeral, wedding, reunion, or convention. Each iteration is putrid. Acrid like hospital coffee. Tight as Sunday-school shoes.

What do you even do at hotels on American highways? Why are you even there?

An American hotel, off an American highway, in an American industrial center, all the empty lots, bad grass nearly dead from the sunshine. Vast slabs of concrete exist, misplaced. There are no lines on them, but surely they are parking lots.

Vacant showrooms, zero merchandise. Lamp posts, not one bulb.

The newer structures—misshapen attempts at something like green-capitalist brutalism. Branded in Helvetica. Crisp acrylic surfaces. Accent walls. Ambient sound. Light that wobbles, wobbles.

In the lobby, water with slices of lime sits in a dispenser on a tableclothed beverage stand, condensation dripping down the dispenser, landing on the soggy tablecloth. Alone, American hotel tap water tastes like a man who can say nothing but his own name fetched it for you yesterday from a well. "Mickey, Mickey," he says, motioning you to drink it. "Mickey, Mickey, Mickey," he says, handing you a plastic cup.

Gentlepeople, the amenities at an American-Highway Hotel are both what Americans aspire to and will just barely tolerate for living conditions.

It is the baseline existence for those with money who are forced to travel, and the lap of luxury for those on vacation from bleaker circumstances.

For others, an American Highway Hotel is the setting for a career. The backbone of a lifestyle.

Comedians with nighttime sunglasses.

Musicians with thinning hair.

Packaging salesmen who enter all rooms aggressively, walk straight to whoever and strike up conversations. "My name's _____. I work in _____."

"You do what exactly?"

"So, let's say you've got a product. You make, I don't know, shredded wheat."

"Cereal?"

"Sure. Cereal. Any cereal you want. Whatever. Lucky Charms. Whatever. Fruity Pebbles. You make the cereal. Do you think you make the boxes too?"

"The what?"

"The what it comes in. The box. Like Trix with the bunny on

the front or the Rice Krispies with the Bee."

"The Bee is Cheerios."

"You proved my point. You've stepped on my trip wire. You've admitted, yourself, that packaging matters. Your packaging. For your product."

"I don't have a product."

"But that's where I come in."

"You make Cheerio boxes?"

"No. But like that. Just air filters. And razor blades. Auto products, primarily. If you've bought wiper fluid in the Midwest in the last 14 years, you probably bought a bottle I sold. I'm the third highest grossing packaging salesmen in all of North America. Last 6 years running. This is one of my last sales runs, though. I'm retiring to Florida. I want to get fat on a beach."

"I could go for that. Any advice? To sell that well? For that long? Without getting bored?"

"Keep notes on everything. Stay in a routine. I use actual paper. If you don't have notes, you'll forget the important stuff, and you want to see the little things. Notes. Paper. That's my advice. And show up on time. Get enough sleep. Simple things. And don't be a pussy. I used to be a wrestler. I used to have to cut weight. When I need to, I can always cut weight."

Of all the people who are sleeping in American-highway hotel rooms tonight, almost none will have a good day tomorrow.

You can sense it on the elevator ride up to your floor. A shaky, lonely endeavor. Your only companion a little lit-up button beside your floor number.

"It's funny you should ask that, Imagination Mary Louise Kelly," I say when I'm on the elevator up to my floor and the doors are shut, and the elevator is ascending. "I too am interested in the American-Highway Hotel."

NOTES ON EVERYTHING

SUNDAY

* Drove to Ohio
* Played some pool
* Talked to a packaging salesman
* Rode an elevator to my room
* Made this note
* I make notes now

MONDAY
6:00 AM

* At Around 2:00 AM. Monday morning. There was a fight in the parking lot. I heard glass break. Sounded like a bottle.
* Got up and tried to see.
* Parking lot was empty when I parted the curtains.
* There is a Bible in the bedside table drawer. There is a bucket for ice.
* Going to Breakfast.

6:51 AM

* Germ ate five biscuits and gravy, a pile of microwaved eggs — scrambled from a bag not the canned kind — two mini muffins and a bowl of Rice Krispies.
* I had a banana and black coffee.
* The lady at the desk asked us what we were in town for. Germ told her we fix wet basements.
* She said that she had a wet basement.
* She asked if he might have time to look at it.
* I can't tell if there's subtext.
* My lead today is actually in Kentucky.

TUESDAY
8:27 AM

✳ Left my notepad in the room yesterday and forgot to write anything down last night.

✳ Sold 44,000 yesterday. Might not need to take notes.

✳ Last night, there was a fight again. A glass bottle broke again.

✳ Again, the parking lot was empty.

✳ If today is baller, this will be my last note. Maybe the positive energy is coming back. Maybe I don't need to listen to the packaging salesmen.

13

"Did you hear the fight last night?"

"Fight?" said Germ. He was shoving biscuits in his face. "No."

"There was one Sunday night too. Or, I guess early Monday morning. I heard glass break. Both nights. Probably a bottle. Did you hear that? A bottle breaking?"

Germ chugged coffee, licked biscuit out of his teeth. "I went to three houses yesterday. Absolutely nothing. Everyone here is crazy or broke or on meth or all three. Were yours on meth. I mean, did they look methy?"

"One family was. My second lead. It was in Kentucky." We were in southern Ohio. Right on the river. Kentucky just a bridge away, so Kentucky was in our service area.

"I have one over there today. Did you sell it?"

"I sold everything I went to yesterday."

"How many did you have?"

"Three."

"You went three for three?"

"Yup."

"Bullshit. What were they. Crawls? Basements?"

"Two basements. One crawl."

"Asshole. How much?"

"Eleven. Twenty. And thirteen."

"Fuck you." He did math. "Forty-four thousand in a day? How much did you get out last month?"

"Forty-eight. The first one paid cash. The third one signed up last night on DocuSign. The second one was crazy. It was in this town called Falmouth. They pronounce it: Foul Mouth. I think. It was an old church."

"Meet with the pastor? Pastors are the worst. They always want a Jesus deal."

"Nah. An old church *building*. A family lives there now. They weren't exactly traditional. There was a woman in her 60s and a man in his 30s and they were married, but just in their minds, not on paper. There were three children. Two boys who were running in circles in and out of rooms. And one girl. She sat with us at the table when we went over everything. She wasn't their daughter."

"Who was she?"

"The man's ex-wife's daughter from another relationship. He married the mother when she was pregnant. Said they got divorced before the girl's birth, but somehow he was raising her."

"What was wrong with the church?" Germ licked his teeth. Gulped more coffee. Aggressively. Pulled at his collar.

"Flooded basement. They just moved in. Had been there two weeks. They had a dumpster out front, and they were tossing out everything that got wet. They had two things going on. One, when it rained, it flooded. But they also had a plumbing leak. There was a pipe that was gurgling water. There was scattered corn and a few lumps of shit on the basement floor right next to the pipe. I asked the little girl what her favorite food was, and she said anything but vegetables. And I said, when I was your age, I didn't like vegetables either. Except for corn."

"I won't eat that," she told me. "If it's part of a plant, I'm a hard no. I won't even say a vegetable's name."

"I wanted it to be her poop, on account of what the adults and boys looked like, you know? Waterproofing was twenty grand. I don't know about plumbing. The little girl said: that's more than Daddy makes, and the man. . ."

"The not father," said Germ.

"Exactly. He said, 'Shut your mouth or I'll knock you out.' But you could tell he had never hit her because she smiled at him and said, 'Knock you out like sauerkraut.' And he messed her hair and I said, 'Sauerkraut's a vegetable's name,' and she said, 'Sauerkraut's food? How do you knock out food?'"

"If he only makes 20K, how'd you get him financed?" Germ pulled his collar some more.

"Dunno. He put 70 on his application, but we still had to find a co-signer. We tried four times before we got it. The fifth person came from down the street in a wheelchair. I'm not sure anyone really knew her. She might've been 100. She looked like an old, greasy white feather, but she had her driver's license, and she was completely coherent. She asked me: 'what happens if I die before they pay it off?'"

"What does happen?" Germ asked.

"No idea."

"What did you tell her?"

"Are you planning on dying soon?"

"No shit?"

"And she said she wasn't planning on anything. But since the loan was for 10 years that it was probably longer than she had. So, I asked: if they can't make their payments, what will you do then? And she said –

"Eat a bullet." She said, "The older I get, the more delicious they look."

"And once we got an approval they wheeled her away. It was like she should have had some kind of banjo theme music. Like a troop of minstrels following with mandolins and tambourines should've come out of their houses and marched her down the road."

"Falmouth?" said Germ.

"Foul Mouth is how I heard everyone say it."

When Germ and I were done eating, we headed out to the parking lot together, but at the exit, just by the front desk, we heard the Desk Lady say, "Hey, wet basement. Y'all okay?"

"Fine," said Germ. "Do we look sick or something?"

"Y'all were hammered. I thought they were calling cops. Y'all kept fighting over money."

Germ and I looked at each other.

"Hammered?" Germ said.

"On what?" I asked.

"Last night," the Desk Lady said. "After y'all were playing pool. You don't remember?"

I looked at Germ. "Have we played pool here?"

Germ looked back at me. "We have not."

The lady looked at both of us. "Hang on," she said. "I take notes on everything. I can tell you the time."

She took a ledger from her desk, opened it up and began to look through. She licked a finger. Flipped pages back and forth. "Duh. Duh. Duh," she said as she perused. "My bad," she closed the ledger. "That's not till Thursday."

I don't know the names of female haircuts, but her hair was dyed nearly white, and I'm sure there was a name for the style of it—the Clementine or the Percival or the Clove or the Slow Gin. Her eyelids almost purple. She had turquoise fingernails. A crystal on a chain. Invisible incense smoke seemed to rise off her.

"You have a note for something that doesn't happen until Thursday?" I said.

"I know, right?"

"But we haven't played pool together and it's Wednesday. Why would you make that note?"

"Duh," she said. "One, you're still staying here. Two, the pool table isn't leaving. Three, tomorrow's Thursday. If it's noted, it's happening. The ledger doesn't lie."

"What happens the day after that?" Germ asked.

She licked a finger. "Well let's just," and she opened the book again and clicked her nails. "Oops," she said. "I'm off. But on Saturday afternoon, a packaging salesman explains cereal boxes to me."

A few families walked through the lobby on the way to breakfast, each and everyone of them seemed barely alive.

"But how do you have notes on the future? What would the point of that be? Who needs to know what happens in a hotel like this on a day like tomorrow?"

She looked to the left. She looked to the right. She leaned into me. "It's so we know how much breakfast to make." She motioned to the quasi-dead visitors loading plates with microwaved goods.

"Do I look at your basement?" said Germ.

"That's my house. I don't have notes on my house. Here, though. . ." she looked around the lobby. "Are y'all telling me you really can't tell? I mean, look at the fucking carpet."

I looked at the fucking carpet. I looked over at the pool

table. At the breakfasting guests. "Last night I heard a fight," I said. "The night before too. And a bottle breaking."

The lady at the desk smiled at me. "Well, Other Wet Basement Man, that doesn't happen last night. Or the night before that either."

"What's your name?" I asked.

"Call me Desk Lady for now. If that changes, I'll tell you."

"Do you play pool with us?" said Germ. "Do you get hammered?"

"Well," said the Desk Lady. "There's only one way to find out."

"Great," said Germ. "I like having things to look forward to. I'm late. I'm leaving. I'll see you both later." And Germ walked out the motion-activated doors and disappeared into the parking lot, moving exactly the way you'd imagine an ex-wrestler would.

The front Desk Lady messed with her fingernails. "Tell your friend not to get his hopes up. My wet basement is just a wet basement. It's not in the notes. But it doesn't need to be. It might as well be written on God's hand."

"It's hard for a wet basement to be anything other than a wet basement," I said. "The one I saw yesterday had corn kernels scattered everywhere on the ground."

"Corn kernels? On the ground? In the basement? Why would that even happen?"

"I'm not really sure," I told her. "But I wish kids ate more vegetables."

FATHER/DAUGHTER TEXT THREAD

Cook: The Desk Lady at this hotel swears she can see the future.

> **Daughter:** Ask her what I'm doing on Saturday

Cook: there's a catch

> **Daughter:** Like the cyclops?

Cook: dunno. What? Only cyclops I can think of is the one that trapped Sinbad and Odysseus.

> **Daughter:** Isn't that two cyclops?

Cook: I don't think so. I think it's like how Batman in the 90's is a different Batman than now but it's just Batman. I saw Christian Bale once. He was tiny.

> **Daughter:** I think most actors are. The cyclops from that fake Star Wars movie where he gets crushed at the end. The one where the guy throws the thing with fingernails on it.

Cook: Krull? Krull is fake Star Wars?

> **Daughter:** They shot lasers.

Cook: Yeah, but they rode winged horses.

> **Daughter:** What matters is how he saw the future.

Cook: I don't really remember. You hated that movie.

> **Daughter:** I liked the cyclops. He traded an eye to see the future, but all he could see was his own death. It

was one of those tricks. Like that Genies do.

Cook: A devil's bargain?

> **Daughter:** Exactly. And that's how it always works with the future probably.

Cook: Did Krull take place on Earth though? Are cyclops just out there everywhere in the whole damn universe?

> **Daughter:** They had humans, too, Dad.

Cook: I hate Sci/Fi and fantasy. There's like four people sitting in basements across North America getting to say what does and doesn't work. I hope their basements leak and all their books get destroyed.

> **Daughter:** That's not good energy. How's it been since you dropped off Harvey?

Cook: Selling tons. But I don't know. The hotel lady says I'm getting into a fight on Thursday with Germ. I have no idea.

> **Daughter:** Well, whatever she sees, it's probably not exactly that. I'm glad you're selling.

Cook: Me too. It'd be stupid to come to Ohio and not make any money.

> **Daughter:** I have to go to sleep.

Cook: Fine. I'll just lay here alone in this haunted hotel.

> **Daughter:** Is it the same as haunted? To see the future?

Cook: I don't know. I guess we'll see.

14

"Do you like codeine?" Germ asked.

It was Thursday morning in Ohio and I was eating my breakfast banana. Drinking my breakfast coffee. Thinking breakfast thoughts. "Codeine?"

"My third lead yesterday," said Germ. "I couldn't get him financed, and I don't know. Have you ever cried in front of a customer?"

"Have *I* ever cried in front of a customer? Me? No. They've cried in front of me. Did you mean, has a customer ever cried in front of me?"

"I've run nine leads. I've sold zero jobs. How many jobs have you sold?"

I had run eight leads and had sold seven jobs. "I'd have to count."

"He has to count."

"So, the financing came back denied, and you started weeping? And they saw it?"

"Shut up," said Germ.

"And they gave *you their* codeine? That's what you're saying to me right now?"

"What was your day? Three for three. Two for two."

"Two for three. I had two little crawls in the morning, and then I had a bigger crawl in the afternoon. The lady who owned the house didn't live there. She and her husband had bought the place and the husband had died, and so she gave the house to her son, she said, and she said she wanted to get it all fixed up for him. Her daughter-in-law was supposed to be there, but she no showed."

"So, you had the afternoon off?"

"Would've been better. I called the lady, and she told me I could just get in the crawl and look around. It was wet and the main beam was under supported. She needed to encapsulate. I called and told her we needed to sit down together and talk about it all, because I think she just had us out because the daughter-in-law thought the floors were 'leaning.' And she told me she was in the hospital, but that I could go see her there."

"I hate hospitals. I don't even like the word. *Hospital*. What the hell other word sounds like that?"

"So, I went."

"To the hospital?" He scooted away from me. "You probably have covid now."

"And I go through security and get back to her room, and she had just gotten a new hip put in but there was some kind of infection, so they had her in there, and they were monitoring all that, and she told me about her husband and kids.

"'My sister had a son killed,'" she told me.

"She said, 'She was setting in the front yard and her boy and the dog were wallering around in the yard, and they got to chasing each other, and they got out in the road. Lived on a highway and the oncoming traffic had no time to break. Boy got struck by a station wagon, and my sister saw it all, said pink mist came off the car, and she jumped out her chair and sprinted to the street to get to her baby. But it was a far ways, and by the time she got there she seen my nephew's head broken open and leaking on the street top, and the dog was eating out what there was on the insides of his skull. Y'know? Her baby's brains.'"

"I want to die like that," said Germ. You could tell he was thinking about dogs.

"She said, 'I think about that every time I hold my son. He's spoiled. I know it. But every time he's unhappy I can't help it. I imagine a dog in his brains.'"

"So, I'm sitting there thinking, like hell yeah. This is my lucky day."

"A laydown," said Germ.

"Oh, a total get-me-done. And I tell her what all she should do, and it's like thirty thousand dollars."

"She cry?"

"No, and neither did I. And no one had codeine."

"Don't knock codeine."

"Germ, she wanted to do everything."

"Everything?"

"Everything. All 30k. For her spoiled son so a dog wouldn't eat his brains."

"How was she paying?"

"Exactly," I said, and Germ laughed, smiled, and sipped juice. "Up until we applied for financing, I thought I was in a dream. Somewhere in Ohio. In a hospital with a stranger. I was on edibles, but that wasn't it."

"Too good to be true?" said Germ.

"Too fucking good to be true, but there's more. She knew."

"Knew what?"

"Knew she wasn't getting financed. When I pressed submit on the application, she started cackling. Just broke out laughing. She said, 'Oh, my god. Look at me.'"

"Oh, my God, look at me?" Germ asked.

"Germ, she didn't have teeth. There wasn't a flower in the room. Everything was gray and depressing, and she had been in the hospital for three weeks and she was lonely."

"She said, 'That's not even my house. I'm just fucking bored to tears.'"

"What?" said Germ.

"She said she knew the house she sent me to. Said it was almost always empty. Apparently, the guy who lives there is a pilot her son used to know. She gets bored. Her son thinks of things for to her do. Today, she's talking to a roofer. Next week, either a walk-in tub or new driveway. She asked me if I preferred asphalt or concrete."

"She gets bored?" said Germ.

"If price were no option. She says it, 'kills the time.'"

"Kills the time? I'd fucking lose it."

"I was kinda impressed. I forgot to ask if the story about her nephew was true."

"I would have smashed the television."

"How quick would a dog start eating its owner's brains?"

"I would have gone to the maternity ward and just started punching babies."

"I guess it could be, like, licking the wound. The dog. Trying to lick the brains back in. Unless it was just really hungry. What is it with you and babies? Eating them? Punching them?"

The Desk Lady hollered, "Did I hear that right?" She stared at us. "Y'all got syrup?" Her phone rang, but she picked it up and hung it up before it could ring again. "And, yeah, I bet a hungry dog would get in there and go to town. Mine gets in the garbage every time I check the mail."

She sat at her desk about 10 yards away. I hollered. "You mean the codeine? That was a while ago in the conversation."

"That's okay," she said. "I liked the rest of the story. I think I'll be that lady when I grow up and need new hips."

"You're nosy," said Germ.

I looked at him. "It's Thursday. I didn't hear the fight last night. Do you think she's full of shit? Or at least a bit wrong? My daughter and I. . ."

The Desk Lady was beside us. Sitting in a chair.

I looked back over at the desk. Back at the Desk Lady.

I stared a moment at her new location, said, "My daughter and I decided that if. . ."

"That if I do see anything, it's probably not exactly what I see," she interrupted. "I don't. I know what happens in this hotel. It's like how a cyclops can predict his own death. I can see all the texts too. And all the internet searches." She looked at Germ but spoke to me. "Your friend has been looking for videos of hotel desk ladies and for pictures of 'short young frisky amateur dyed white hair nudes.' He found one that's close." She looked back at me. "I don't know if he shows it to you. It's not me, though. We just look a lot alike."

"Bullshit," said Germ.

"He took a screen shot," the Desk Lady said, leaning toward me. "Think he'll share the syrup? I mean, I know, but what's your take."

I looked down at my phone, at my texts from my daughter. 'Whatever she sees, it's probably not exactly that.'

"I don't know," I said. "He might. But I've got a house to go to." I looked at Germ. "Feel free to text me if you want. I don't want to think about this anymore," I said. "I wanna go make some fucking money."

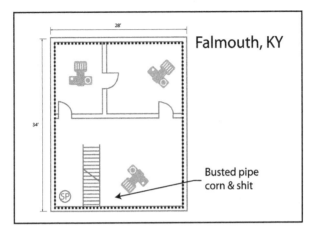

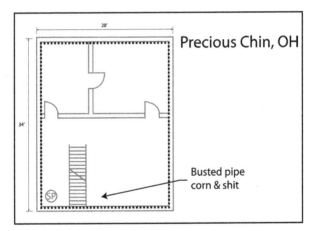

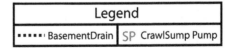

15

What ended up being my last lead in Ohio was in a town called Precious Chin. You won't be able to find it on a map, or at least I haven't been able to find it on a map and I don't have my company phone anymore, so I can't look up whether or not I'm wrong. But there is definitely a text thread in my daughter's phone where I say, "I'm going to a place called Precious Chin," but where was it?

I know right before that I was in Kentucky, and I was sitting in my Prius, stalled in traffic on a bridge over some river, looking down at greasy water when my phone rang.

It was the main office and I answered it.

"The Cook," said Mortimer. "Down in Ohio," he continued. "Cooking up deals."

"Hello, Mortimer." I watched a bird land on a stump and take a bubbly, white shit on split, beige bark.

"I'm seeing the numbers. I'm loving your numbers."

"It's been a good week."

"Looking at the leads left. Already talked to Germ. Ohio hasn't been so good for him."

"You can't have beginner's luck forever."

"Not everyone can be a top guy," Mortimer agreed.

I watched the riverbank below. A quasi-vagrant sat in a lawn chair with a fishing pole, smoking a thin cigar, his hat brim pulled low.

"To that end," said Mortimer, and he paused and the man on the bank reeled in, cast out, relaxed in his chair, and a plume of smoke scat away from under his hat brim. "Numbers as a whole in Ohio have been a little less than optimal."

"Whose numbers?" I had run 9 leads and had sold over 100k. My close rate was over 70%. My average dollars per sale were twice what I'd ever seen, and I had made over $10,000 in less than four selling days.

"The only numbers there are. Team numbers."

"Team numbers? Who gives a fuck about team numbers? I mean, it's KPI. I don't care about anyone's numbers but mine."

A LinkedIn-flavored silence ensued. Mortimer drew breath. "At the end of the day, we are a team, obviously, our friend Darby is on the hot seat."

"Hot seat? Darby? How?" The man on the bank raised up from his chair, wandered toward the tree line and took a piss. His back was toward me, but there's only one reason to stand that way.

"It was his call to send you and Germ to Ohio together. Told me you needed it to get out of your slump. And Germ needed it to pick up polish."

"I heard you sent Germ. Either way, I've sold almost everything I've touched."

"Germ is struggling and it was a team decision to send him."

"Let him struggle."

"That doesn't sound like a top guy thing to say. Have you checked in with him at all?"

"Top guys will definitely watch a boy beneath them struggle. We've talked every morning. He's working on a self gen that I doubt he'll convert. A wet basement for our Desk Lady. She might be able to see the future. Well, at least in the hotel. I'm hanging up now, I need to drive. I'm driving."

"Wait, wait. I've got it pulled up. It's pretty simple. You and Germ have five leads left between the two of you. If you can get out 30k more, the whole trip will be a huge success and Darby will be fine."

"I have one lead left. And Darby can fuck himself. Exactly zero percent of me coming here was my idea."

"One lead?" said Mortimer. "Not what I'm seeing. I'm looking at it right now. I got the system pulled up right now."

"You can't pull up where I go," I said. "You can only pull up where you want me to go. I pitched a job in the hospital yesterday. I think my customer was infectious."

"Do not cancel your leads. That's not what top guys do. Drink fluids. Rehydrate."

"Yeah, feeling pretty off," I coughed into the phone. "I'll get a test and let you know." I coughed again. Cuh, cuh.

"Cook," said Mortimer. "You do not have covid. No one has covid."

"Talk later."

"Cook."

I hung up the phone and watched the fisherman on the bank walk back to his chair, slouch down and start fishing, and I thought about whether or not I should just go back to the hotel and wait for night.

A few of the stalled cars began to honk, and the man on the bank looked up at the bridge, and our eyes locked briefly, and I turned my head and stared down the river so he didn't know I was watching him and the river rolled out to wherever, and I wondered how much of the water in it had been in a crawlspace I fixed, had been moved by a system I sold.

How many gallons from how many sump-pump discharges had pushed water out from under a house I'd been beneath, down a long, buried pipe, to where it bubbled up from the yard, drizzled down to the gutter, and made its journey to the river I was now parked above? How much of that water was supposed to be destroying a house instead of being a dirty river for vagrants to fish in?

Here are how my leads went that day:

The first one, in Kentucky, was normal. Small job. A sump pump in a basement and some extended downspouts. Not much to say. It was a single gentleman who served in Vietnam. Not in combat, though. Some kind of logistics. He explained it, but I didn't understand him. He was old and white and his hand shook when he held a pen.

The third one was two kids I didn't bid.

But the second one, in Precious Chin, was in an old Church building. A family was living there. The basement had flooded. When I pulled up, they had a dumpster out front, and they were tossing away everything that got wet. There was a man standing inside the dumpster, redistributing garbage. "Just moved in," he told me, once he realized who I was. "First rainstorm and this shit." He wore a newsboy cap, a white tank top and overalls. He had glistening, broad shoulders, and garage-grade tattoos. He fished a green bandana from his back pocket, removed his cap and wiped his face. "It's always something," he said. "Or at least I can't remember the last time it was nothing."

I looked up and down the road. "You haven't seen me before, have you?"

The man considered me. Put his hat back on. Folded his bandana and wiped his mouth. "We go to the same high school or something?"

"No," I said. "The neighborhood just looks familiar."

"Hell," he said. "All shitholes look like Precious Chin."

He climbed down from the dumpster, shook my hand, and we walked the concrete path toward his home. "This didn't used to be a church did it?'

"Sure did. Not for a while, though. I remember, when I was a kid, you'd see ladies in big ass hats coming up this path on Sunday morning. Dresses to match and everything. I don't worship. But my grandma used to make me come. Still looks like a church, though, I guess."

"I looked at a church in Kentucky like this two days ago. Also converted into a house. Also with a flooded basement."

"Think they just built 'em with the same problems?"

"I guess."

Some smells should be painted green, just so you can try to avoid them—rusted sewage, standing gray water. The water had come up 14" across the whole basement, which is just enough for most things to get destroyed. There was a line of dried foam and bits of debris against the block walls. Scag all the way around. The way you fix it is you jackhammer all the way around the perimeter, bury a drainage pipe to catch all the groundwater, and replace the concrete you removed. It's expensive, and it wasn't their only problem.

There was a plumbing leak that would have to be looked at by someone else, and I wasn't sure how it fit into the problem, but there was a busted pipe emptying on the basement floor, and there were lumps of shit and scattered corn.

"It's crazy," I said to the man in the overalls. "I've never seen two properties so similar."

"Basements don't usually leak like this?"

"No. Basements almost always leak like this. At least eventually." I pulled up the diagram of the house in Kentucky and the pictures. "Look."

They had the exact same footprint. The same obstructions. The same symptoms and root causes. The stuff was all different. Clearly they had different stuff. But both of them were 28X34 rectangles. Eight by sixteen concrete block, three-part foundation. Seven blocks high. One above grade. Same size joists. Same size sill. The thing was probably a hillbilly church schematic that you used to be able to order off Southern Ohio Christian FM Talk Radio.

"Not gonna lie, that makes me feel a little better. To see another one like this. I thought God just hated me."

We finished up looking at the basement, and I put together the proposal, and we sat at a table in the kitchen, and it was me and the man and an older woman and a little girl. Deeper in the house, two boys ran in circles in and out of rooms.

"Were the kids here when it rained?" I asked.

"Rained?" said the lady with us. "I pray for rain. No one prays for it to fall like that. Deluge is what that was. Biblical. I thought: I'll swim if I have to, but what would the point be?" The woman looked off at nothing. "I thought, if the water comes up over my head, I'm just gonna open my mouth and fill up and sink to the bottom and stay there."

"He can fix it though," the man said. "Right? It don't have to flood again, right? And get all our stuff?"

"You can fix it," I said. "But. . ."

"There it is," the woman said. "But. You hear that word, and you're about to spend money. Bout to have to tell your kids they can't have the food they want."

I looked at the little girl. Her hair was in braids. Her eyes aglow. "What do you like to eat?" I asked.

"Anything but vegetables," the little girl said. "I won't even say a vegetable's name."

"What about insurance?" said the woman. "Does insurance

do it?"

"Not usually," I said. "But you should definitely reach out to them once you have the proposal. They might cover something. I've had a few customers have insurance come through. It depends on the language in the policy."

"That fine print," said the woman.

"Yes, ma'am. The clauses and such."

"And without insurance?" the man said. "If they won't pay for it, how much would it cost us?"

I looked at the proposal. I didn't care if I sold them anything. I was tired and wanted to go home. "Twenty thousand, eight hundred and four dollars, but I can do it for twenty thousand on the nose."

"That's more than daddy makes," said the little girl.

"Shut your mouth 'fore I knock you out," said the man.

"Knock you out like sauerkraut," said the little girl.

I stared at that little girl a long while. Whose child was she but God's? And why was all her stuff in a dumpster now? "Sauerkraut's a vegetables name," I said.

"It is?" said the little girl. "How do you knock out a vegetable?"

The only difference between the houses was the final outcome. Again, the man lied about how much money he made. Again, we had to try several co-signers.

But the last co-signer we tried, her name was Louisiana Betty, and they brought her down from up the street in a wheelchair. She was ancient. Looked like a greasy black feather wrapped up in a shawl.

But she was coherent, and she had a license, and she co-signed the application, and we waited for the answer from the financing company, but even before it came back, Louisiana Betty sort of knew.

She whispered, "Ever notice how the older you get, the more delicious bullets look?"

The sky was gray. Tumultuous clouds hung like bundled gauze. The father was outside in the front yard with me. "It bet not rain," he said and was still sweating.

When the application came back declined, I stood there with my phone in my hand looking at the notification from my app that said the company we financed through would send the customer a letter explaining why they'd been denied a loan. I showed him the message.

"I don't know who else to try," he said. He wiped his face with his bandana. "We'll have to do some talking around."

"I'm sorry," I said. "I wish I could do something else." I gave him my card. "Call if you get any ideas, and I'll call you if something changes on my end. I wish I could fix it for you. I'll try to figure out something."

He pocketed my card and motioned to his friends, and they turned Louisiana Betty around slow, and the neighborhood seemed to walk away with her, and four gentlemen with horns—two trumpets, a trombone and tuba—and a fifth with a bass drum, wandered out from houses and fell in line behind them all, and they played some long, drawn out dirge, and slow, dulcet notes hung in the air of Precious Chin like fingers of fog, and everyone who was outside in their front yards and in the streets hung their heads and dragged back into their houses and closed their doors, and Precious Chin seemed to go to sleep like that, as though some poisoned haze had chased life from the world.

The last lead I ran that day was the last lead I ever ran for that company.

It was a young white couple who had just moved into a flipped house in a black neighborhood. They came to the door wearing pandemic masks, and they had a plexiglass-covered screen door they stayed behind, but I could see, in the room behind them, two open laptops, each broadcasting a Zoom meeting. You could sort of hear grind culture language echoing off the walls.

"We can't let you in," the man said to me. "Unless you have a mask."

I had a mask. I took it out of my pocket. I put it on.

There was some kind of floppy, mixed-breed dog that walked up and sat down with them.

"I don't want to come in," I said. "What's wrong with your house?"

They looked at each other, and then they explained to me that they'd only recently moved in and just wanted to make sure everything was okay.

"Smelling anything?" I asked.

"I don't know," the woman said, "what would it smell like?"

"Something you'd know if you smelled. Seeing anything?"

"Like?" said the man.

"Cracks," I said. "In the walls. Or do any of the floors feel wobbly."

The woman looked around. "No," she said. "No."

"Any scattered corn?"

"Scattered corn?"

"Your home's fine," I said.

"Thank god," the woman said. She needed no convincing beyond that. She petted her dog. "Boujee needs this eye procedure." She held her dog's head toward me. "You can probably see it." I saw nothing out of the ordinary.

"It won't be cheap," the man said. "Expensive," he said down to his dog in some goofy voice. "Expensive girl. So expensive." He rubbed her coat.

I was in Cincinnati in some gentrified strip. There were a few un-rescued houses that stood in various states of decay, but other than that, all the homes had been gutted and flipped.

"You guys ever hear of Precious Chin?"

"What's that? Something dogs get?"

"No. It's a town. Here in Ohio. I just came from there. I was with a family. Their house flooded a few weeks ago when it rained."

"It was crazy, the rain," said the man.

"They just moved in too," I said. "Their house is pretty much garbage now. It's unfortunate for everybody."

"Oh, bummer," said the lady. She quit petting her dog. "Bummer. Bummer. Bummer."

"Do y'all believe in energy?" I asked.

"Energy?" said the lady.

"Like if you put out good energy, do you think you'll get back good energy?"

"Oh, we're all about energy," said the man. He turned to the lady. "Karma," he told her.

"Oh, Karma," she agreed. "Thaaat energy. Absolutely."

"How's y'all's credit?" I asked.

"Excuse me?" said the man.

"For good energy. Think y'all could hold a 20k loan?"

The lady said, "What?"

"Well, to co-sign," I said. "For that house that floods. Right now, they're down in Precious Chin, throwing away all their stuff and its sprinkling. Can you imagine? It's terrifying. I mean, they already have a little girl who will never say the word sauerkraut again."

"Is that even legal?" asked the man.

"I have no idea. But they don't ask a lot of questions. It's all run through an app." I held up my phone. "I scan your ID, and you answer a few questions." I held out my hand. "I just scan your license."

The woman said, "But what if they don't pay?"

"I guess your dog would go blind," I said.

The man pretended to think. "That would really mess up our credit, bro." I knew he'd say bro eventually to me.

"It'll get better," I said. "I can tell. You guys will always be successful. Abundance mentality."

"We can't."

"Why?"

"Because we can't?"

"Fine," I said. I put away my phone. I didn't need my app. I looked at all the houses. At all their signs. I didn't have anything to add. I stepped off their porch. "Best of luck with your dog's eyes," I said. Then I got back in my car and drove back to the hotel.

EMERGENCY ALERT

SILVER ALERT in Shelby County, Indiana. Man last seen getting out of a crawl space with a cowboy hat on. Walked into a neighboring cornfield and never emerged. Answers to Dan. Might be carrying a bullwhip. Overly interested in green laser light. You probably don't need to proceed with caution. Will no longer eat octopus.

16

"I doubt they'd tell me yes," the Desk Lady said. "I'm keeping y'all out of my basement."

She and Germ and I were loose around the pool table. They'd mixed codeine syrup with Mountain Dew and were trying to learn to play pool. I'd eaten 200 mgs of Delta-8, and I could smell the house in Precious Chin in my clothes.

Germ took his phone from his pocket. "Do you have a license? We could run you and find out."

"But what does it look at?" The Desk Lady held up her Mountain Dew. "Dirty, dirty, dirty," she said and sipped it.

"Your scores," said Germ.

She swallowed and you could tell she was numbing out. Her lips looked too heavy for her face to hold comfortably. "What scores?"

"The score of your whole life," I said. "Every dollar they've ever seen you spend. Every dollar they've ever seen you make. How much you owe. How much you've saved. Whether or not you've been to prison. The score says what you can borrow."

"Ooh. Can you look up my scores and tell me?"

"Not really. Not the way we have it set up. I used to sell cars, and when I did that, I could get reports and see everything. Wanna know what gives most people bad credit?"

"God damn it," Germ said. He had missed some shot at the pool table and made like he was going to break the cue over his leg.

"Germ, you're aggressive," said the Desk Lady. "Did he show you the screen shot?"

"I don't have a screen shot," Germ said. He held up his phone. "You can check my fucking camera roll."

"Can I check your recently deleted folder?" the Desk Lady said. "Can I check that?"

"Fuck off," Germ said.

"Are there more Mountain Dews?" I sort of looked around. "I'm thirsty."

The Desk Lady got up and walked to the desk, reached

underneath, grabbed a Mountain Dew from a small refrigerator, and moved back toward us, opening the bottle.

"What gives them bad credit?"

I took the bottle from her, had a long drink, and set the Mountain Dew on the table. "Student loan debt," I said.

"I never went to college," the Desk Lady said.

"I wish I didn't," said Germ. "I owe seventy-five thousand for a degree I don't even use. I pay three hundred bucks a god damned month. By the time I've paid for everything, I'll have spent like a half million dollars to get a teaching job I quit after three years. Or, I don't know," he reached down to the pool table and spun a ball, "it at least feels like a half million."

"Do you need a degree to do what y'all do?"

"No," I said. "I used to be a professor. I did something like this when I was twenty. Quit. Went to school. Got a master's and started teaching college. And if I'd just stayed doing this, I'd be able to retire in my 50s. I'll never retire now. But I've read the classics."

"Classics?"

"Oh, they're nothing. The books they used to tell you to read. They called it the canon. Higher ed is like selling windows in a neighborhood where it rains bricks. And the customers are like: but it rains bricks. And you're like: but that's why you need the windows. If you don't have the windows, you can't see the bricks, and if you can't see the bricks you can't stop the bricks. And they'd be like: but how does that stop the bricks? And you'd be like: motherfucker stopping the bricks is your problem, but you can't know how until you buy and replace a ton of these windows."

"I changed my mind," said the Desk Lady. I don't want to see. I don't wanna know what some person in some app thinks my score is."

"It's not a person," I said. "It's Manhattan Money Math. They plug you into an equation that tells the future of your money." I sipped my Mountain Dew. "Money's a story. That's what they say these days. Money's a story. Data is a story. It's all stories. Even when your shit's under water. Then it's a whole other story. The story of your wet fucked up shit. And the story of loads of money to spend. And that story, the story of money, they say that's the greatest story ever told."

"Like the Bible?" Germ said. He came over to the table where the Desk Lady and I sat, and he picked up the dirty Mountain Dew and had a sip and set it back. "Isn't that what they say about the Bible?"

"They used to. But it's money now. They quit being dishonest. Ever sold to a Hindu?"

"A Hindu?"

"A Hindu," I said. "They're usually Asian. I guess most of them are from India."

"Like a Muslim."

"Absolutely not. You went to college? Muslims don't work as well because Muslims and Christians have the same God just different prophets. It works better if it's two groups that don't have the same deity."

"I've sold to all types of people. Just not in Ohio."

"You really haven't though," I said. "There's lots and lots of types of people. Groups within groups. You have only sold in Indiana. I have sold in Indiana and Kentucky and Ohio, and I'm not sure how many more types of people I've sold to than you, but it at least sounds like more, and I would never begin to say I've sold to all types of people, because I know that different places build houses different, and I don't think a Protestant homeowner with a crawl space is anything like a Protestant homeowner with a basement and maybe two Protestant basement owners become entirely different things when only one of them is lefthanded."

"Salesmen talk fast," said the Desk Lady. "So many words. The guy on Saturday also tells me the history of windshield wiper fluid. How he gets to that from cereal boxes I have no idea."

"Fine," said Germ. "I haven't sold to all types of people. And I don't know if I've sold to a Hindu or not, because I'm sure that if I saw a Hindu and Muslim side by side I wouldn't be able to tell you who believed what, but I don't get what the hell you're getting at."

"Fine. Then do you think Muslims and Christians believe in the same god? Do you think they believe the same things? Go to the same source when they need answers to questions?"

"No. I don't think so. It's totally different."

"Then working off that premise. . ."

"Is it a premise?" said the Desk Lady.

"When you sell to a Muslim, do you believe in their god?"

"No," said Germ. "I'm kinda Christian, I guess."

"Like on Christmas at least?"

"Yeah, on Christmas. Easter. I'm baptized, and circumcised."

"You are a fucking idiot, Germ."

"I looked it up," said the Desk Lady. "Here are the synonyms: assumption, presumption, thesis. So, yeah." She sipped lean. Gurgled it like mouthwash. "Premise."

"So, you don't believe in their God, but did you believe in their money?"

"Their money?"

"Their money."

"It's money. What's to believe about it?"

"You have to believe it's worth something. How many people in the world do you think don't think money is real?"

"What?"

"How many people in this world do you think spend money?"

"Are you asking me, how many people in this world do I think spend money? Is that what you're asking me?"

"Yes."

"I mean aside from I guess a few people still using like seashells or trading blankets. . ."

"Okay, the seashells would still be a kind of money, but it doesn't matter. Just roughly? How many people do you think still trade blankets?"

"Like fucking hippies, I guess," said Germ.

"Hippies isn't a number, but do you think there are more people who trade blankets or more Christians?"

"I mean. I don't know."

"Guess, motherfucker. You literally have two choices."

"Christians then."

The Desk Lady clapped a little. "Ooh it's already started."

"Okay then. So, money is a better story than God."

"God's not a story, is he?" said the front Desk Lady.

"Do you and Germ hook up?" I asked. "If it's written on God's palm, then those words are a story." I held my hand out to Germ. "Show me your phone."

"Fuck no," he said. "And fuck you."

"No, Germ," I said. "Fuck you and fuck you," and I snatched up my Mountain Dew and took a chug.

I was furious, and I was thirsty, and I'm an alcoholic—rage-chugging all dramatically—but when I lowered the bottle, and looked at Germ and the Desk Lady, I realized I had made a terrible mistake. They were moving so slow. And my hands were so far away.

"How'd it get so purple in here?" I asked.

For the slightest instant, I could feel the fuzziest of emergencies.

And then. . .

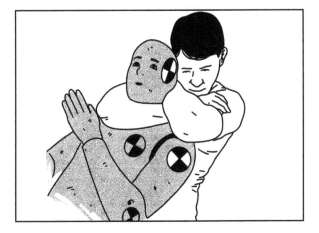

17

They put me in a squad car with a thick plastic back seat and every turn they took, they took hard as fuck. I sat mashed on my handcuffed hands.

"It doesn't hurt when you do that," I said.

They leaned into a left and my skull popped against something and my wrists squelched in their cuffs.

I have regained consciousness in a cop car on several occasions. I was only mildly confused.

They made a few more hard turns and then I was in a hallway being dragged by my arms. "Where'd the car go?" I asked. I'd also lost my handcuffs. "Who the fuck has my hands?"

No one answered my questions.

They deposited me in the drunk tank for processing, and I woke up in a small cell with two cousins who'd been popped for fentanyl. One of them had a half torn off ear. The other one kept rubbing his shoulder. I stretched a little and accidentally made eye contact.

"You been out a minute," the one rubbing his shoulder said. "You was mumbling about money. What they get you for?"

"Don't know." My head was thumping. "Prolly PI, I guess. I was loud in the hotel. Screaming a little. At a friend. And then whatever."

"See," said the bit-eared one, "we was in our own goddamned house, and we wasn't doing shit."

"The cops wasn't even looking for us," agreed the other one.

"They was looking for a dude we know. And I've talked to him, but I ain't seen him. He's got a murder warrant, but I've heard his side and I don't know. I wouldn't call him honest, but he didn't seem like he was lying. They shouldn't been looking at our shit at all."

"What'd y'all have?" I asked. I couldn't quite think.

"Shit," said the bit-eared cousin.

The other rubbed his shoulder. "A little blonde."

"Bruh that sounds like we out there raping babies. He don't know to call it that." He locked eyes with me. "Starts with F and ends with ill."

"Yeah, but hunting murderers though."

"Y'all had it though? Right? They found it? Like, they got in your house and it was there?"

The one stopped rubbing his shoulder, and the other sort of began pulling at his mangled ear.

"I don't know," I said to them both. "Sounds to me like you're fucked."

They shuffled us to a room where we talked to a judge on something like a Zoom call, and the two cousins went wherever fentanyl boys go, and I got put in gen pop at county. They dressed me in orange and gave me a roll of toilet paper, and I got marched down dimly lit concrete corridors, passing through security checks and going up and down elevators, seemingly charging toward the center of a bunker where I didn't want to be.

They set me up in a two-bed cell, and my bunky was a young rapper named Trap Tre.

"Take risks and prosper. That's what Trap means," he sang when he introduced himself. He was sitting on the bottom bunk holding a Styrofoam bowl in one hand and a spork in the other, and he smiled when I entered and said, "You just in time for snacks." He'd been cooking in a microwave with ingredients from the commissary, and I put my toilet paper down and looked around the cell. "Hold out your hand," Trap said. He stood up and walked over and began stirring his bowl of food. "I'll give you a taste."

I looked at my hand, covered in jail germs, and held it out and Trap put a spoonful of whatever it was on my palm. "That's how we do," he assured me. I think it was ramen noodles with imitation bacon bits and melted Velveeta spread.

It shimmered, and I was queasy, but jail friends are hard to come by, so I tossed the goop in my mouth, and it was like eating a slug made of cheddar cheese. "Flavorful," I said and licked my hand. I chewed but didn't need to.

Everything in the cell was fluorescent-lit and smelled like Metallica-concert urine. There was a 2'x2' window in our cell, and you could look out onto the hills of Ohio.

Trap was a college dropout who had played college ball. He thought the Earth was flat and he wanted to talk about Dr. Sebi and Nipsey Hussle.

"He could fix AIDS and shit with like roots and shit, and Nipsey knew that shit and was talking it. And that's when they killed that [gentleperson]."

Trap and I were as close as bunkies can get in one day of lockup. We read David Baldacci and Michael Connelly out loud to each other, books we got from contraband libraries the long-termers had stashed under their bunks, and Trap taught me jail-shit etiquette.

"You hang the blanket over the door," he told me. "That way I know and stay out on block."

He also let me know when they would let us use the phones, and as soon as time came, I called my wife.

"Jackass," she said, after agreeing to the charges. "How's jail in Ohio?"

"I mean, I can only compare it to Texas."

"Germ called. He tried taking all the blame. Says he's sorry for the sleeper hold."

"I don't remember that at all."

"You're not supposed to be home until tonight, so I won't be mad until tonight. Hopefully it won't be too expensive. At least you weren't driving and at least it wasn't booze. You're not going to have to go on a bender are you?"

I've never been able to drink for less than two weeks in a row. Once, I woke up in a hotel in Monterrey, Mexico and the last thing I remembered was being in Texas. "No. I'm great. What's work think?"

"That you have covid."

"Know when I get out?"

"Tomorrow morning. You'll have to get a ride back to the hotel, but Germ got your stuff put in your car. He said the Desk Lady helped him get in your room. And he says he's staying in

Ohio. He said you'd understand."

"No shit? Tell our oldest daughter the Desk Lady was right."

"She already told me. Did you know she thinks you're cursed?'"

"She's not *wrong*," I said. "She's just got parts wrong."

"That's what I told her. I said your father's just like this. No use trying to fix him."

That night Trap and I watched the sunset.

"Say it again," I told him.

"Flat," he said.

"The sun just set," I said. "We watched it."

"That's what they taught you. The world is a disc."

"And the sun?"

"A disc."

"And the universe?"

"A computer program."

"I grew up in Texas."

"So?"

"On the Coast."

"So?"

"I have seen thousands of sailboats disappear on the horizon. Like thousands. You just stand on the beach and there they go."

"I'd have to see for myself," Trap said. "You can't take a prisoner's word."

Trap had gone to Youngstown State on a football scholarship. He majored in African American Studies. "I bet you think I majored in bullshit," he told me.

"No," I said. "I think almost everyone majors in bullshit. I have a degree in communications and creative writing. That's a degree in, like, talking and telling stories. I might as well have written my thesis in fingerpaint."

Trap gave me the top bunk. I was lying there looking at the ceiling, and he was lying in the bottom bunk and looking at my mattress, but we were talking to each other like we were front to front.

"Think I should go back?" he asked. "Get a degree? I got a

buddy who wants me to do a cell phone scheme with him. He gets phones from here and mails 'em to Turkey, and he's got a guy who sells 'em there for like five times what you pay here. Maybe I should do that."

"I don't know. When I was your age I didn't have a degree. But I have one now, and I sell foundation repair. And there's like 20 salesmen where I work and some have degrees and some don't. I'm the seventh best salesman there. Another college graduate is about to get fired."

"I just want money," said Trap. "When I get out of here, I wanna get my money straight. Get a house. Get a Lexus. I don't know. Maybe I'll invent something."

"You should invent a machine that takes awkward out of the air. A Lexus? I used to sell cars."

"How would it do that? That sounds way too technical. I don't really do science. I do deals. Like here's how the phone scheme works: you get people to buy cellphones on credit over here, then you mail those to my dude in Turkey, and he sells them for like six times what they're worth here. Ever sell a Lexus?"

"I sold a used one. It had a heated steering wheel, so it basically had everything, because they don't give you one of those unless you go high trim. It was so expensive, I tried to talk them into a new car instead. I mean, not a Lexus, though. The husband didn't like the idea."

"I mean, yeah. You can't just drive anything. And if you can, you should always drive Lexus."

"I bet you also like Dodge, Chevy, Audi, and Acura. If the universe is a computer program, those cars and Lexus is in your source code."

"Yeah. That's literally every car I like."

"White dudes want pickup trucks. Black dudes want muscle cars. Asians dudes want Toyotas, and they always haggle with cash. You'd be like: this one is twenty thousand, and they'd be like: I'll give you fourteen grand cash if you do it today. But dealerships hate cash. And you're never getting a discount like that."

"Fuck Toyota," said Trap. "Those things always smell weird."

"A Lexus is a Toyota," I said. "An Acura is a Honda. An Infiniti is a Nissan. A Buick is a GMC. A Kia is kind of a Hyundai. Ford is only Ford, I think."

"Like, those cars make those other cars?"

"Yeah. Those cars make those other cars, or they'll have like the same engines and the same transmissions and the same everything but panels and knobs."

"No shit?"

"No shit," I said. "The universe is a computer program."

"And the motherfucking world is flat," he agreed.

TEXT THREAD W/ WIFE

Cook: Got my shit from hotel. Headed back. Will call when on road a while.

> **Wife:** Was it different not drunk?

Cook: I don't know. I met a rapper. He was a flat earther. I'll send you links to him on YouTube. His name's Trap. He has a video or two. They're pretty good. He says the universe is a computer program. And if Trap thinks so, I think so.

> **Wife:** Do you think the Earth is flat too?

Cook: I do not.

> **Wife:** You're lucky your jail stories make me laugh. You're an idiot.

Cook: Do I smoke too much weed?

> **Wife:** No. You drank a bottle of Codeine. Pull your shit together and quit feeling sorry for yourself and come home and take care of your family.

Cook: Will you tell me if I smoke too much weed?

> **Wife:** I can't tell when you're high. How about I just tell you if you're spending too much money.

Cook: But then you could tell me how much money I get to spend.

> **Wife:** You only buy weed, Diet Coke, Cigars, T-shirts, books, and guitar strings. You don't "need" any of those things. You're 43 years old. You shop like a 15-year-old boy with a Pink Floyd shirt on.

Cook: I'll call on the road.

Wife: Do not be drinking when you get here.

Cook: I'm not drinking.

Wife: If you are drinking, stay in Ohio.

Cook: I'm not drinking.

Wife: Then come and take your daughter on a walk. She hasn't left her room in three days. And please take her somewhere other than the cemetery.

18

I had a missed call from Cowboy Dan when I was in jail, and I'd never missed a call from him. I'd never taken a call from him either, which made it seem important, so I called him as I was crossing into Indiana, just to see if he was okay.

"Hey, old man," I said when he answered.

"Hey, sick puppy." His gravelly voice seemed to grind through the phone receiver. "How's the covid?"

"I ain't got fucking covid," I said.

"I know. Something's in the air. You hear about Darby?"

"What about him?"

"Got arrested for swerving, finally. Taken in last night. These things come in waves. I've been around long enough to have seen. You still in Ohio?"

"Nah, just got out. Just crossed the line." Ohio and Indiana look about the same in most places, but all the signage is different.

"Pass through here," said Cowboy Dan. "You probably have to anyway. I'll send you my address. It won't take you long. I want to show you something."

Cowboy Dan sent me his address, and I looked at the map, doing my best to watch where I was going while looking where I'd be going.

"You gonna show me how to find ghosts with my laser?" I said. "I missed that part of the speech."

"Oh, that shit's not real. I just tell that story to scare the kids. They'll set up their lasers in a shitshow and start seeing whatever it is they want to see. Did you try it?"

"A few times?"

"Yeah, but I bet you don't even feel like your time was wasted? No. It's not about lasers. Not at all. Wanted to show you how they used to do it. Just in case you've never seen one."

"Seen one what?"

"You'll see when you get here."

About a half hour later, I pulled into Cowboy Dan's. He lived on a four-acre tract carved out in the corn fields. "In a few weeks," he said, when I stepped out of my car. "I'll be able to see the road from here."

"The privacy is nice though." The home seemed to spring out of the cornfields like it grew that way one season after having exceptional rains.

"Oh, I'm used to being cramped in."

"What am I here to see?" I asked.

He adjusted his hat. "We're getting under my house."

Cowboy Dan lived in an old Victorian with a cellar door cut out into the side of the house, and he led me down steps, pulling a light bulb cord on his descent, and the stairs wobbled beneath us as we moved, and when we got to the cellar he motioned like scattering seed or paying tribute to the land, and he said, "Anything look peculiar?"

I had heard about what he had, but I had never seen one. They weren't so rare that they were all on some historical registry, but I suppose someday they will be. On a map of Indiana or the United States or whatever. The location of every house built on a stack stone foundation. The foundation walls were fieldstones on their sides. You've maybe seen something similar stacked at the edge of properties, or used as something like fences in the sheep fields of Ireland.

Each of the stones was about the size of a pizza box, and shimmered with condensation, and they were stacked in some quasi-haphazard fashion, laid to fit as best as possible and held in place by gravity and time and the craftiness of their configurations. You could smell broken stone and standing fresh water. Moss and algae, but not mold. A foundation of rock-stacked walls.

"You've got a stack stone foundation," I said.

"Well, in this house. I have three. One here. One in Florida. One out west. This one is stack stone. You can't fix these. A laser can't show you anything."

I ran my hand down the stone walls, crammed my fingers into the spaces between the rocks. Above us, thousands of pounds of lumber and furniture and whatever else is in a house, sat hoisted erect. "What are you gonna do with it?"

"Absolutely nothing. Just gonna leave it. It'll be the last house I get under. Can you imagine stacking up all these rocks. There's thousands."

"At least."

You could hear water slurping. I looked at the stacked stones. "I come from Texas," I said. "We didn't have houses like this, I don't think."

"What were they like?" Cowboy Dan asked. "The old ones?"

"I don't know," I told him. "I didn't know about houses, and I don't think I ever really looked at them. Old or new. I can't really remember."

"Well, there's time," said Cowboy Dan.

I took one last good look at the stacked stone walls, wobbled into place by whatever primitive masons had wandered through the land and settled it. It felt like being in a cave. There should have been stalagmites all around our feet, stalactites bonking us on the heads, and we wobbled back up the stairs and into the daylight.

After that, I got in my car and drove home with the radio off.

There were combines on the road. The corn would get cut soon. It had dried out in the sun, stood brown and anemic, rattling back and forth in the breezes, and the combines would sweep across the state in the coming days and weeks, and the landscape would be razed of corn and soybeans and sprawl open and lay prone to be covered by snow come winter.

I zipped along in my Prius with jail on my skin, dreaming of taking a hot shower and taking a shit on a toilet not made from metal, but when I got home my oldest daughter was waiting at the back door for me, and immediately the energy felt off, because it sucks being embarrassed.

"The Curse of Juan Pablo strikes again," she said.

"I don't think that's what it is," I told her.

"Then just good old fashioned distorted energy."

"Are you mad at me?"

"Why?"

"I don't know. I let you down. Or I let down the magic. I don't know."

"No," she said. "You said it. You sold, like, everything."

"But I got arrested."

"Think how much worse it would've been if you hadn't taken Harvey though, but I remembered something."

"What's that?"

"His hat," she said and lifted it toward me.

"You think if he gets that I won't get arrested anymore?"

"Absolutely not," my daughter said. "But he's on the way to Texas."

"What does that have to do with anything?"

"The next time we go," she said. "We can take it to him then."

"Thank god," I said. "I thought you were going to tell me I had to go now."

"No, no, no," she said. "Right now we're taking a walk."

"Fine," I said. "I can put off the shower. But you're going to have to wait a few minutes."

Then I went inside, didn't hang a sheet on the door, sat in perfect comfort, and shat out whatever Trap had fed me.

19

The next day, I made two phone calls:

The first one was to Mortimer and he was absolutely stupefied and breathing heavily, and you cannot hear someone pulling their hair through the phone, except somehow I could hear him on the other side of the line—way up there in the frozen north, in some maple-syrup colored, fire-lit study—pulling his hair with his free hand probably staring into flames.

"What the hell is happening in your Goddamned nation? You're collapsing. Cowboy Dan is MIA. I just got word that Darby's locked up with a DUI. Germ mailed in his tools. Absolutely embarrassing team numbers. What the hell happened in Ohio?"

"I sold a shit ton of jobs and got covid. Then I came home. I saw the silver alert on Dan this morning. I didn't know about Germ's tools. It was only a matter of time with Darby. You'll always have Kipler."

"Did Germ say anything to you? Tell you where he was going. Was he doing drugs? I can't believe I listened to Darby."

"Sending Germ was your idea."

"Yes, but a team decision. If I was wrong, Darby should've told me. I guess he was always just drunk. It doesn't matter now. We'll have to pull together as a team. I've got your calendar completely full for the week. I need your Ohio numbers to follow you home. We have to have those kind of numbers from someone. Someone has to step up. To grind. To pick up slack. I'm already having to head back to Indiana once the snow stops falling. I do not want to have to go back out in the field."

If you've never had the pleasure of hearing your boss suffer on long distance when you don't care about your job, I recommend it. They can never eat you, but when they're on long distance and you'd like to get fired, they can't even show their teeth.

"I can't work, man. I'm sick. It's crazy. I'm not sure you've heard. Something's going around. Like, the whole world has it. They've closed schools. We're supposed to wear masks."

"Top guys don't get sick this much. It's ridiculous. You've already had it, and I'm wearing a mask."

When I'm on the phone long enough, I'll distract myself with chores, so I walked into the kitchen and began putting away silverware, because I wanted Mortimer to hear me ignoring him.

"That's what I said to the doctor." Ptang! "And do you know what he told me?" Pah-klang! "Said it's probably a different variant." Clank, cling, clang. "I've got my shots. At least both of them, but it isn't as bad this time, and I guess that's what they say. It won't be as bad. I'll let you know when I'm negative."

I tossed a few more forks, and that finished up the silverware, so I went to hang up my phone.

"Cook. Cook. Cook." Mortimer said, quickly at the end. "You have to be well. I need you to get well."

"Oh, I will," I said. "Getting better all the time." And I hung up the phone.

The next call I made was to the hotel. I wasn't exactly worried about Germ, but I figured I'd check in to see if the Desk Lady knew if he was okay and to get a little more clarity or closure. An Irish Goodbye is when you leave a party without telling anyone. I don't know what it's called when you pass out and never talk to someone again, so I looked up the phone number and called, and a woman's voice answered, and I said, "Is this the Desk Lady with the wet basement?"

"I've been waiting for you," she said. "I got sloppy and didn't write down the time, but I knew the call was coming. Oh," she said. "No. Wait. It's just this pen's out of ink." It sounded like she stuck out her tongue and licked her pen tip, then I heard the pen against paper, back and forth really fast. "Completely out."

"Me too," I said. "What the hell happened? When did the cops come?"

"Oh, that? You broke a bottle, passed out, and we put you on the pool table, and I think one of the other guests called the cops. When they got here, you puked purple. Dirty. But they didn't realize what it was. Germ told them you hadn't been feeling well, and you told Germ you'd kill him and scratch the name off his grave."

"Have you talked to him? Germ?"

"Ugh. Almost every day. He and that goddamned packaging salesman hit it off. They're both wrestlers. They've been showing each other moves in the courtesy gym. They're both staying in the hotel right now, and they're racing to see who can lose 20 pounds the fastest. I don't know. I feel like they're the same person. They're sleeping in the same room. The packaging guy is paying. I see them together, at the same time, but I keep waiting for them to merge or something. Plus, they're both in love with me. Poor guys. They streamed *The Notebook*. Twice. It's one of the reasons I want to change jobs. I need new energy."

"Why would you leave a job where you always know what's going to happen? I feel like you could really use that to your advantage somehow."

"No way," she said. "It doesn't feel ethical, and I only have notes through next week. I think it's out of my control. You call me one more time though. Did you know that? From Texas. In a few days."

"How the hell could I know that, and why the hell am I in Texas in a few days?"

"Second part: no idea. First part: maybe on accident? Hit the wrong number in your call history? Dunno. But you tell me to tell you to go to Texas. The note says: 'Tell Cook to go to Texas. Tell him he made me write it down.' I guess I get a new pen."

"That's it? I don't say why?"

"Nope. That's what I got. There's a smiley face by the note though. Don't know what it means. But it's like a really good smiley face, and I usually can't draw anything."

"I'm never calling you again," I told her.

"Not even if you think of a real good reason?"

"There couldn't be a good enough reason to think of."

"But you'll be thinking about it."

"I will not. I will not be thinking of reasons."

"Okay," she told me. "Talk soon."

And she hung up the phone and I swear to god I nearly called back immediately to get the last word in, but realized at the last second how much power that would've given her. It would've been like: shazam.

And I think I was staring in disbelief at the floor with my phone in my hand when my wife entered the room.

"Did Carlo Rovelli email back?" she asked. I think she was excited for me.

"Carlo will never email back," I said. "It was the Desk Lady. At the hotel."

"Do you have a crush or something?"

"Absolutely not. That's Germ's imaginary girlfriend now. This time next year, he'll be able to tell you what her license plate says."

"Ew."

"Yeah, I'd say it sounds worse than it is, or is better than it sounds. But it's definitely a concerning pattern of behavior."

"Is that why you're cussing at the carpet?" my wife asked.

"Cussing at the carpet?"

"Yeah, dad. Cussing at the carpet," my youngest daughter said. She was sitting on the sofa about eight feet away from me.

"Where the hell did you come from?" I asked her.

She had a small turtle in her hand about the size of a cookie that she was cleaning with a toothbrush. "Serious, bruh? I've been sitting here this whole time."

"I was cussing at the carpet? Whose toothbrush is that?"

"I thought it was the way he prayed," my youngest daughter said to my wife. She turned the tiny turtle over and toothbrushed its belly. "When he does that."

"I mean, you might not be wrong," my wife said.

"I just sit in here and cuss at the carpet?" The toothbrush was orange, so it wasn't mine, but I had a very strong suspicion it belonged to somebody. "Like every day?"

"Oh, yeah. At least once a day. Yeah."

"God damn it," I said. "I think I have to go to Texas."

"Right now?" my wife said. "You're just gonna drive to Texas?"

"No," I told her. "Gotta wait until at least tomorrow." I got up and walked to my youngest daughter and looked down at the toothbrush.

"It's an old one," my youngest daughter said. "It's not yours."

"Why?" my wife said.

"Because it was under the sink with old toothbrushes."

"No," said my wife. "Why are you going to Texas tomorrow?"

"Because the first thing I gotta do," I told her, "is take my tools to the post office."

CRAWL SPACE TEXT THREAD #3

Mortimer: Alright gentleman. It's a beautiful day to be out here in the field. I can't wait for all of you to start posting all your sales. We have houses to fix and customers to take care of and money to make. Let's fucking go!!!!!

Kipler: Gentlepeople.

Mortimer: Good catch, Kipler. Way to pay attention to the details. Exactly. Gentlepeople. Gentlepeople indeed.

Kipler: What can I say. Top guys doing top guy things.

Cook: Kipler, were you there when Cowboy Dan used the laser to find ghosts?

Mortimer: This isn't what this channel is for. Your laser isn't for ghosts.

Kipler: I mean, kind of. I don't really know what he was talking about. Remember how I wanted snacks? I checked your satchel, and borrowed some of your expensive candy. And by the time he got to the actual ghost part I wasn't really paying attention because the lights were out and the laser was spinning, and he was holding his measuring wheel over his head like a staff. He looked like a god damned wizard. I've tried it though and didn't work at all. I just sat beneath a house watching the dust in the light trying to see whoever I was supposed to see in it, but I didn't see anything but dust and cobwebs.

Cook: Kipler, don't send texts that long ever again. It's like you're about to mail explosives.

Mortimer: Yeah, uh, Kipler. I'm going to have to agree with Cook here on this one. People who send texts like that usually send mail bombs. But it's still okay. You're still a top guy on this team.

Kipler: You do realize you should be saying top person, right Mortimer?

Mortimer: Top-person catch right there, Kipler. Top-person catch all day long!!

20

There are two ways from my part of Indiana to my part of Texas. One route dices through Kentucky and Tennessee and the other one cuts down Illinois and Missouri. Both ways you go through Arkansas before you hit Texas, but if you're headed to Terre Haute, you're headed toward Illinois.

My route was decided for me.

I've gone both ways. I prefer neither. Through Illinois is about a half-hour quicker, but both routes are between 18 and 19 hours, and anything that long feels like 100 hours either way, but I would've blamed Harvey if he'd added time to my trip—screaming at him those last 40 minutes on Texas highways—and I needed to reduce negative vibes. To undistort myself.

It's why I was taking him the hat.

Through Illinois, down to the coast of Texas, is 1,212 miles. My 2019 Prius model XLE gets about 50 miles to the gallon and has an 11.3-gallon tank. It also has lane keep assist, blind spot detection, and smart cruise control. It does not, however, have Apple Car Play or heated seats, and I'm not entirely certain that my vehicle is any better for the environment than a traditional combustion-engine vehicle of a similar size. The places where they mine for battery minerals get strip fucked, and Texas, where they hoist oil from the earth, is beautiful though pocked with derricks. Every time we figure it out, the future shows us our failures. I get good MPGs though. In theory, if I had a strong bladder and a non-anxious disposition, I could make the trip in three pit stops, but I am not the type of person who can drive like that. I have to get out every few hours. Stretch my legs. Talk to strangers.

I stopped at the same convenience store I stopped at when I was with Harvey, only they were out of Delta-8 gummies so I had to get a vape. It was okay though. I figured I'd practice blowing smoke rings with cannabis vapor the whole way down.

I know how to juggle. If I could only blow smoke rings and whistle with my fingers, I would be the coolest dad alive.

The stop at Terre Haute was quick enough. I knocked a few

times at the door but no one at the house answered, so I put Harvey's hat in the mailbox and headed on.

I passed through Illinois with its flat cornfields and pounced nothings. Through Missouri, with its throbbing pornography advertisements and monstrosity churches. Through Arkansas and its Ozark half-mountains. And down the Texas coastline, filthy with energy production—refineries, derricks, and so many windmills you can't even count them.

I basically drove straight from my house to the house JP had died under, because I figured if I was going to Texas for any reason that would be the most likely reason to go.

But when I pressed park and sat in my Prius and watched the house, I realized, "That's not the same fucking house." I hit my Delta 8 pen and tried to blow a ring, but it came out wobbly and crooked, and the house that sat where the house that killed JP once sat looked pristine.

"It seems to me, Imagination Mary Louise Kelly," I said, "Someone has knocked it down and started over." It made a lot of sense. Who wants to live on top of where someone died?

I messed with my phone, trying to think of something to search for an answer to, and I sent a few texts. Maybe I felt relieved. Sometimes, the worst thing that can happen is getting what you want.

I couldn't tell for sure, but I didn't think the new house sat on a crawl. "It might be impossible for me to get under you at all," I said to the house. Would I need the laser in the trunk? Should I have just mailed it to Mortimer along with everything else? He obviously hadn't gotten my package, because I hadn't heard from him about it yet. I wondered if he was in the field. I sort of imagined an open laptop in a crawl space, Mortimer on the screen trying to read relative humidity through the internet.

Anyhow, there I was in my old neighborhood in Corpus Christi, TX—the town where I went to high school—a beautifully ragged place that smells like salt and sulfur and looks like a knife fight is bound to happen in the sunshine.

The city hugs a coastline, and every Saturday and Sunday,

windsurfers pollute the bay with their sales akimbo, spiriting along the white caps, and in the distance, refinery steam streaks the sky. Selena died there. The leader of Heaven's Gate was born there. Its second most famous musician is The Reverend Horton Heat.

The street I was parked on dead-ended into Ocean Drive which runs along Corpus Christi Bay and is peppered with giant houses and aged condominiums—everything weathered by salt spray and sunlight.

Along the seawall, there is a large statue of Jesus standing in the front of a boat, presumably calming the waters to keep our shrimpers safe, but a few months after the monument was erected, a drunk driver passed out and smashed their car into the boat beneath Jesus' feet.

Corpus.

I considered the clouds. Texas bay towns have busy skies. Every color you could know of, every kind of cloud they make, exists perpetually. They heap and streak and stride and mottle. Blue haunting infinity above them.

All of my work stuff said Indiana on it, and I didn't quite know what excuse I might use to go to the door. I hoped no one was home so I could just slip under unnoticed, but there wasn't a crawl door out front, and there was a car in the driveway, and I didn't want to jump a fence and sneak inside, because at some point, no matter your intentions, it just feels like breaking and entering.

I got down and went up. Walked the sidewalk, stepped gingerly onto the porch, lowered my eyes and rang the doorbell. It chimed out the opening notes of "Dreaming of You," and a short woman who looked like she made a chocoflan for every funeral she ever attended answered wearing a Puebla dress and no shoes. The house smelled of Fabulosa and wedding cookies and cumin and sage. There were sugar skulls in the wind chimes and eucalyptus bouquets on the mantle.

"Are you Jehovah's?" she asked when she saw me. "I already have a church and it lets me celebrate birthdays."

"No, ma'am. I used to live a few streets over. . ."

"Are you selling magazines?"

"No, ma'am."

"Cable?"

"No."

"No one takes the paper." She raised her voice like she thought I couldn't hear her. "Are you an identity thief?" She had glasses on a chain that hung from her neck and she lifted them up and set them on the bridge of her nose, pushed them back toward her face as far as they could go and squinted at me.

"No, ma'am, I was just curious to see when this house was built. I feel like it was always here, but it looks different than when I was a kid."

"It is different," she said. "The old one got too old. But we weren't going anywhere. You can walk to the bay and Selena's grave from here. Everyone parks here on the 4th of July."

In Corpus Christi, 4th of July fireworks go off above the bay. They fire them from a beached battleship called the USS Lexington. It's from WWII, and I have visited its pinched quarters and had a throbbing anxiety attack, but that was back when I drank and before I got used to being in low-clearance crawls. Either way, I could never be in the Navy. "I haven't been here for fireworks in years," I said. "I've been to the grave though. It's like a bench, right?"

"I guess it looks like a bench, but I don't think they want you to sit on it. I never have. Was that your question?" she said. "About the house?" She motioned back into the home. "I have cookies in the oven."

"Pretty much," I said. "I was just also kind of curious. And you might not know. But does this house sit on a crawl?"

"What?"

"Sorry. The foundation. Do you know if it's a crawl space. Or. . ."

"No," said the lady. "What a weird question to knock on a door over. It's the other kind."

"Basement?"

"No."

"A slab?"

"Slab?"

"A concrete slab foundation."

"That's the one," she said. "A man died under the last one, so when we rebuilt, I told them I didn't want a house anyone can die under. I had people come and burn sage, you know. It's a whole ordeal. A kid in the neighborhood told my daughter about it, and she had nightmares for weeks."

"Y'all lived here then?"

"I was a child in this house," she said. "I've always been here."

"Do you know how the man died?" I asked. "The one who died underneath it."

"My husband knew. He didn't exactly tell me. I used to ask him and he said 'you don't want to know that,' but I guess there are only so many different ways you could have died down there. I mean, it's not like a shark bit him in half. I always figured either electricity or bad air. I don't think anything fell on him." She sniffed. "My cookies smell done. You're sure you're not an identity thief."

"No, ma'am."

"Then I guess welcome back to the neighborhood." She frowned at me and closed the door and I stood there for a long while looking at the peephole from the wrong side, but the porch still smelled like cookies.

"It's funny you should ask that, Imagination Mary Louise Kelly," I said as I dragged my way back to the Prius, but I couldn't think of a question for her to ask me, so I just went to the trunk of my car and got out my laser, and I set it up on its tripod in the middle of the road and cranked it on and fired a single green laser beam at the house JP died under, and I wasn't expecting to see a ghost, and I wasn't expecting to end a curse. I was just sending a beam of light. And I watched the clouds overhead a while, and then I ran the laser line down the mortar line of the home, and the whole thing was level.

The dot showed nothing.

So, I turned off my laser and broke down the tripod, and

threw everything back in the trunk of my car, and thumped the hatchback closed, got in and figured I'd head straight home.

What a disappointing journey.

The Prius has a push button start, so I hit that then hit my vape pen, and rolled toward Ocean Drive chewing on my thumb tip and humming to myself. I hung a left and drove north with the bay on my right-hand side, watching the sun glint off the water. Even on bad days, sunlight on the water doesn't suck, and if I was going to be water, I'd want to be the kind sun shines off.

I guess about a mile down the road, I looked into my rearview mirror, and realized maybe the curse wasn't broken. "Sweet Imagination Mary Louise Kelly," I said.

There was a police cruiser behind me and the cop had pressed a button near his collar and was talking to dispatch, I think. I can feel it when they run my plates. I'm a veteran of police interactions. It's like your rearview mirror twitches. And I'm not passing judgment. They have a hard job. I'm not weighing in at all. All I know is that I am like every other Human American Motorist in that when a cop drives behind me, my butthole muscle feels different.

I don't like getting pulled over, but I especially don't like getting pulled over on busy streets, so I put my blinker on and made to turn into a neighborhood. My plates were from Indiana, and my car was legal, but when you have out-of-state plates and a cop is behind you, you think the worst.

I tucked my vape pen deep beneath my seat—Delta-8 is legal in Texas, but surely having it in a moving automobile is frowned upon—and I pressed a few buttons on my steering wheel, and my car called the wife, and she picked up and said, "You in Texas?"

"I am," I told her.

"Did you go to the house?"

"I did."

"And?"

"Well, one it's a different house. And two," I came to the intersection with my blinker going dink, dink, dink, dink, dink, and I began to pull into a neighborhood an old girlfriend had lived in. There were a few alleyways that jagged and sputtered behind the streets, and I thought I could maybe lose the cop in old side streets that I knew in my youth, but I wondered what all besides the house that killed JP had changed, and I also remembered I was driving a Prius, and police chases aren't really about MPGs. "Anyhow, there's a cop driving behind me."

"Wait, wait, wait," said the wife. "What was two?"

"I don't remember. I got a lot on my mind."

"You drove all the way to Texas to go to a house that doesn't exist anymore so that maybe you won't get in trouble anymore, and you already have a cop driving behind you?"

"What can I say? I'm efficient and consistent. Just pumping out distorted energy."

"You know what really distorts energy?"

"Posting bail?" I asked.

"Posting bail," my wife agreed.

In the rearview, I saw the policeman reach for something, and his siren chirped at me, a quick bleat.

"Hear that?"

"All the way to Texas," my wife said. "House isn't even there."

"I love you," I said.

A long pause ensued.

"Honey?" I said.

"Idiot," she told me.

OCT. 1, 20XX

Dear Mortimer,

I have enclosed all the tools you have given me except for my laser and phone which will come in a subsequent package. Please consider this my immediate resignation, and please tell Kipler he owes me money for the candy he stole.

Sincerely,
Cook

21

I watched the police officer come to my door, his right hand on his gun butt, his left hand extended like I was a dog and he thought I might sniff it. "Good afternoon, sir," he told me. "Do you know why I stopped you?"

"Is it because I shot my laser at that house?"

"Excuse me?" the officer said.

"Nothing."

"Can I see your license?"

"Sure. Can I reach for it?"

"Go ahead."

I reached for my wallet and fished out my license, and I passed it over to him, and he began to peruse it.

"I wasn't speeding. Or anything," I said. "Though in Indiana, I got a ticket once for going the speed limit. Are my plates legal?"

"When's the last time you were in Indiana?" the officer said.

"The day before yesterday. I just got in. I think I slept a few hours in Arkansas last night. It might have been Missouri. Just at a rest stop though. I'm not staying in a hotel for a while. They're spooky places."

"I'll be back in a moment," the officer said, and he kept his hand on his gun butt and backed away slowly from my Prius, watching me with one hand pushing the button of his Walkie-Talkie and the other hand ready to draw and fire. He spoke a few words and heard a few replies. I could hear the talking but I couldn't make out any of it. And then he was moving back toward my window.

"Sir," he said, "I'm going to have to ask you to step out of the car."

"Should I put my hands up and everything? I mean, I've done this before. Are we going in? I can just go get in the back of your car."

"Eventually I'll have you do that," he told me. "But first I'll need to put you in cuffs."

"Hands behind my back then?" I said.

"Hands behind your back," he agreed.

Now, I've been arrested a few different ways, but the best way they can arrest you is when they're looking for you but you aren't mad at them. Like, I had no idea why he'd want me, or what I'd done. "Did my boss say I stole my laser?" I asked.

"You keep talking about lasers. Are you on drugs?"

"Absolutely not," I lied. "It's a tool. A survey laser. It's in the trunk. I told my boss I had covid, but I don't have covid." By this time I was sitting on the asphalt with my hands cuffed behind me, watching the officer go through my Prius. "If you're looking for something," I said. "I'll tell you where it is."

The cop didn't answer me, and he didn't find my vape pen, and then he put me in the back of his police car.

"Are you feeling my positive vibes?" I asked. "Is there anything you need?"

"Shut up," he said.

"Of course," I said. "For you, anything."

We drove along Ocean Drive in the same direction I had been headed, and we passed the Jesus statue a drunk hit once and made our way downtown. That's where their jail is. I've been more than once. The first time I ever went to jail was in Corpus Christi. I was drunk at a Whataburger and back in the day, there was a microphone that the cashiers would talk into. And I remember being in a Whataburger. And I remember grabbing a microphone. And all of a sudden I was in jail screaming at some woman who was taking my wallet away from me.

The holding cell in Corpus Christi is a single cell gen pop, and once they force you through the front gates, you get redistributed to a huge room with two bathroom stalls — the same metal toilet / sink combination that all jails use — and there are steel benches that line the walls and there are folks sleeping on them. It's hard to call the guys in drunk tank "inmates." It's super transitory. You can leave there and graduate to worse facilities, but half the time you're just there to get your picture taken and sober up. Most of the people leave walking. I figured when I left, I'd go have a hamburger at this place downtown that has surfboards for tables. I was pretty sure I was just passing through.

In the large cell, there was a payphone, and hogging up the payphone was this 19-year-old kid. "Baby, if I could get up out this prison, I would fly up out this prison. Be with you, boo. Be with you."

He whispered to her like that a while, and then when that phone call ended he made a collect call to Louisiana and started talking to some other girl the exact same way.

After a while, the door buzzed open, and a detective called my name. He looked like a real detective, and I got a bad feeling. "Is this about Cowboy Dan?" I said when they asked me to follow them. But they didn't say anything, and I felt the fluorescent light tighten around me.

They took me to an interrogation room, and I had never been to one of those. It was a little green 10X10 room and I think that's where they take you when they plan on keeping you a while.

What had I done?

There were two officers. One was portly and Polish and the other skinny, Hispanic and gay. The Polish one was Detective Durks and the Hispanic one was Lieutenant Martinez.

"I could take guesses, but I don't really know," I thought a second. "Does it have anything to do with the woke couple in Ohio?"

"Excuse me?" Durks said. "The who?"

"I tried to get them to cosign a loan for a family in need. But they wanted to get their dog a surgery instead. I guess it would be fraud, but we didn't do it, though. It was just an idea."

"When were you in Ohio," Martinez asked.

The light felt heavy. The 10X10 seemed to constrict. "Like a few days ago."

"Before or after you were in Indiana?" said Durks.

"Before."

"And why were you in Ohio," said Martinez.

"For work," I said. "I look at houses. Like foundations. I told the guy who arrested me about my laser and all. I stayed at a hotel. Is there a reason I'm here?"

"Can someone corroborate that? Like tell us when you were there?" Durks said.

"There's a lady at that hotel who can tell you when I was there and where I'll be tomorrow. At least sometimes."

"Why were you in Terre Haute yesterday?" said Martinez.

"I dropped off a hat. At a house. My daughter made it. The hat. Not the house. For Harvey."

"Harvey Corker?" Martinez said.

"Yeah, that sounds about right," I said. "I only heard his last name once. My daughter made him this hat, and the last time I saw him was when I dropped him at that house. My daughter made me take him. He thought it would help him quit cussing. I don't really know why. Is he okay?"

Martinez and Durks looked at each other. "We'll be back," Durks said.

They stepped out and shut the door behind them, and I could hear talking through the door, but nothing I could make out. Cops are good at letting you hear them without letting you understand them, but after a bit they came back in.

"Come on," Durks said, and I walked with the two men to a different holding cell, and they opened it and let me in, and I sat down on a metal bench, and there was someone sleeping on the bench in front of me with their face to the wall, and there was a little white guy with a giant bruise on his forehead.

He looked at me for a while. He sort of tapped at his forehead where the bruise was. "Will you touch this and tell me what you think?" He motioned to the guy sleeping. "I asked him and he told me something about computer programs or something. I feel like it's soft. Does it feel soft?"

I could see his bruised skin move as he pressed his finger against his forehead. Like sinking in. "I don't know what I'd be comparing it to. I mean, I don't know what it normally feels like."

"Just compare it to the rest of my skull," he said. "Like this over here," he said and pushed on the side of his head, "feels different than this part." He pushed on his bruised forehead again.

I made like I was about to touch his head.

"Don't touch that boy's head," the person sleeping on the bench said toward the wall. "He's lying. I did it and he grabbed my hand and licked it. That's how he got the bruise. It wasn't there before. I hit him. Hit him hard."

"God damnit, why'd you tell him that?" the white boy said. "It's like the best jail joke ever. I almost wanna get arrested just to do it to people."

"That's sick as fuck, man. Try that shit in Ohio and you'd be dead. Youngstown prisoners'd fuck you up. Why could you possibly want to lick a stranger's hand?"

"I was just in Youngstown," I said. "I thought the prisoners were pretty okay. I didn't try licking anyone's hand though. I licked my own hand I guess. Ate some Ramen off it my bunky gave me."

"That's how they do," the sleeper said.

"Takes risk and prosper, I guess," I said.

"Bullshit," the sleeping prisoner said. "You know my lyrics. . ." and then he turned on the bench and it was fucking Trap Tre. All the way down in Texas. "Motherfucker," he said when he saw me, his voice completely disappointed. "This is the worst computer program in the whole world. I was excited, do you understand that? I thought somehow I had fans all the way down here."

I couldn't believe he was in front of me. "But I am a fan," I told him. "Kind of."

"You are 40 years old. That's old enough to fuck my mom. I barely know you and you've let me down twice in the last six hours."

"How the hell are you here?" I asked him. "It's weird as fuck."

"I didn't think it was weird when you got arrested where I live," said Trap.

"Y'all be knowing each other?" the white kid said. For whatever reason he was still pushing on his bruise.

"I don't live here, though. I just used to live here," I said.

"You don't think it's a spooky coincidence?"

"Man, you're the only reason I'm here," said Trap. "Came to see about your fucking sailboats or whatever. Got out and jumped a bus straight to Texas, because after you left I just kept watching the sunset and thinking about it, and whatever you're right. I couldn't even see across the whole bay. Just boat after boat disappearing. I drank a whole bottle of Fireball just watching it. I figured if you were on the beach you could be drinking. Apparently, that's not the case. Now I'm all arrested. I feel like my whole life is a lie. You know how many people I've been telling the Earth is a disc too? You know how many motherfuckers are gonna know I'm wrong just as soon as they see me? I won't even have to say anything. It'll show in my eyes."

"Yeah," I said, "but you also tell them the universe is a computer program. And look. How could it not be?"

Trap thought a minute, I could tell by his face. Just thinking. "How d'you mean?"

"How else would we be here together? How else could this happen? Has to be like, programmed in."

He nodded. "It is a bit random."

"Nah," I told him. "It's not random at all. You got out of jail and came to Texas. I quit my job and came to Texas. Just two people in a computer program headed to Texas for sure. So what? You're wrong about it being flat. But you're right about the other thing, and all that means is you're right as much as you're wrong, and that's better than most."

"You quit?"

"Yup. Mailed my tools in and everything. All I have is my laser and my phone, and once that's all mailed in it's over for sure. Fuck that place. Fuck those people."

"But you got your phone still though?"

"Yeah. I mean not on me. They got it wherever my shit is."

"At the desk? Like was it in your car or in your pocket?"

"My pocket. I think. I can't really remember."

"If they got it up front, leave it for me." Trap sat leaning against the wall, fully at ease on the metal, jail bench.

"What?"

"I told you about the phones. I can mail it to Turkey. My guy will front me. He sends cash Venmo. We're tight. We've been through it."

"But it's my work phone."

"But didn't you say you quit your job?"

"I did."

"And didn't you say 'fuck that place?'"

"He said that," said the white boy. "I heard it. I heard you say it."

"I said fuck that place," I said.

"Well," said Trap, "seems to me if you don't work there and you don't like them, then you shouldn't care whether or not they get back their phone."

"Trap," I said, "are you trying to close me?"

"Of course I am," he said. "I'm an artist, and artists are salesmen. How else could you get people to think they should pay attention to your imagination? Also, why the hell did you leave here for Indiana? Man, I might not even go back to Ohio. Winter is bullshit. You're crazy."

"Oh, you know," I said. "My wife missed the snow."

"I really do think this spot is softer," said the white kid pushing again at his bruise. "It might not have been before, but maybe after you hit me it happened."

"Well," said Trap. "Be careful what you wish for."

"But I didn't wish for nothing." He kept pushing and pushing.

"Then be more careful when you lie."

WIFE TEXT THREAD # 2

Cook: Got my stuff and getting out. But I won't have my phone on me. I'll be home in like a day and a half.

> **Wife:** Dude, you are embarrassing. Handle your shit? And why won't you have your phone.

Cook: I have to leave it for someone?

> **Wife** Leave it for someone? Who the hell would you be leaving it for?

Cook: I can't tell you and you wouldn't believe me.

> **Wife:** You can't get arrested again for at least five years.

Cook: Fair.

> **Wife:** And if you aren't here in a day and a half, just don't even come home.

Cook: I'm on my way. I'll be there. Don't answer calls or texts anymore from this number.

> **Wife:** I married white trash.

Cook: Well yeah. But it's not like I didn't tell you that. Plus you have half white trash kids now, so don't look down too hard at us.

> **Wife:** Embarrassing.

Cook: I'll drive safe.

> **Wife:** I guess we'll see.

22

The next morning Detective Durks came by alone and told me I was getting out.

"We had to hold you until everything cleared. Your friend Harvey is in big trouble."

"Oh, he's not my friend," I told him. "We barely even know each other."

I was supposed to check in with a district attorney in Indiana by phone once I got back into town, but there weren't any charges pressed against me, and I didn't have to post bail.

The lady at the processing desk had my personal belongings in a plastic bag, and she was looking over my paperwork. "You stayed out of here a minute," she told me. "I tell everyone when they leave, I hope this is your last time. But I haven't always said that. I don't know how well it works, but just in case: I hope this is your last time."

"How long have you been here? Working?"

She didn't have to think. "Coming up on thirty years and thirty years is all I'm doing. Four months left. Then I'm retiring home to Alabama. You can't keep me off the Gulf. It sounds terrible, but I live for hurricane season."

"Thirty years at this desk?"

"This whole time," she handed me my stuff. "Sign here." She pointed to a form.

"Think you were the one who processed me out last time? I was 17. It was like 26 years ago."

"Maybe. I'd've been a baby. But, in four months, it'll all be a memory, and I don't think I'll revisit it."

"I was an asshole first time I got brought here. I yelled at everyone. They put me in a restraining chair. I'm sorry."

"I do not remember, and I do not care, and four months from now, in Alabama, if I ever think about any of y'all I'll just drink a margarita and ride around in my sailboat in the sunshine. I don't really know how to sail, but I'll learn. I'll leave the dock and just go until when I look it's nothing but water."

"Sounds nice." I took all the things out of my bag, turned

on my phone and sent a few texts to my wife. "There's a guy in here from Ohio. In the cell I was in. Can I leave this for him?" I motioned to my phone.

"Leave him your phone? Why would you do that?"

"He needs it for something. I just gotta make a quick call and then you could like, I dunno sneak it into his bag."

"Absolutely not," she said. "It's not allowed."

I opened my call history and hit the number to the hotel in Ohio. The Desk Lady answered and said, "See."

"Oh, whatever," I told her. "Is your pen working?"

"Let's seeeeeeee," I could tell she was writing. "Ooh," she said. "I just made a perfect smiley face."

"I know," I told her. "Now, right next to that, do me a favor. Write down that I told you to tell me to go to Texas."

"I'm not your secretary," she said. But I knew she was writing. "But I guess you won't be able to do this for much longer."

"About that," I said. "You should really get a ledger with a lock on it. If you're gonna stay at that job. You don't want everyone to know what you know. You know?"

"I told you," she said. "I'm not doing this job anymore. I'm not staying here."

"Maybe," I said. "Maybe not. But I've been thinking a lot. You should look around. Is there a book with a lock on it? Like anywhere around there?"

The phone was silent a while. "You motherfucker," she told me, and I hung up my phone.

"Listen," I said to the woman in the jail, "didn't you say you were leaving this job soon?"

"I did," she told me.

"And didn't you say you'd never think about this place ever again?"

"I did."

"So, doesn't it seem like it's not that big a deal. That you can just put this phone in that bag and it won't matter because four months from now on a sailboat with a margarita in your hand looking back, you'll only see water. This won't be a memory at all."

She smiled. "You criminals are all the same," she told me. "You're sweet when you're talking and when you're talking you're lying."

"No," I said. "Everything I told you was the truth. You'll be on a sailboat, and none of this will ever matter."

My phone rang. The lady and I both looked at it.

"Don't answer it," I told her. "The woman calling wants an answer I don't have."

"What's her question?"

"She wants to know how she got a notebook with a lock on it."

"How'd she get it?"

"I'm not entirely certain," I said. "But I think I just vibed it right."

We both watched the phone buzz and jingle, and the screen lit up and then the notification chimed that I'd missed a call. "It won't matter," I said again.

The woman was silent. She took a deep breath. Then she opened Trap's possessions bag and gave Trap my phone.

I got my Prius out of impound and started back up the coast on my drive home. The Texas coastline is guarded by barrier islands that carve up Gulf waters into little lagunas, and the land that emerges between the lagunas and the Gulf is filthy with windmills that spin slowly, the white blades going round and round at the top of tall metal columns, and their spinning makes energy and the energy is fed back into the grid.

When they first started placing them, there were just a few, and they were marvelous structures that seemed to presuppose the future. They seemed to spin up there and their spinning seemed to say: I am the future come to save you from yourself.

But I bet you anything someday a Cowboy will stare up at them for the last time, and they'll be obsolete. They won't spin or make energy, and no one will know how to fix them. And someday after that, they'll eventually fall down.

And so as I drove, I tried to count them all, or to see them all. So that no matter what happened, we would be entangled somehow, and maybe our paths would cross again.

We would spin, or we would spin again, or we would never spin again forever.

I fished my vape pen out from beneath my seat, and it took me a few tries but I huffed out a perfect vape ring, and I felt like I became a better father just watching it dissipate. I could juggle. I could blow vape rings. I couldn't whistle with my fingers yet, but maybe I don't want to be that loud.

"Funny you should ask, Imagination Mary Louise Kelly," I said as I drove amongst all the windmills. "You see, I've thought about that a lot. Juggling is fine. Whistling with your fingers might even be better. But blowing a vape ring? A perfect vape ring? That's the real sign. Because that's the real job of every good father: to perform and old trick for a new world."

But that might be the only time I ever really blew a good one.

Now, I changed companies about a year ago, and I hadn't thought about Harvey or the nameless grave or Germ or Ohio for months, but then one day I was checking my leads, and I had one coming up in Terre Haute.

We don't usually look at houses built before 1920, and we don't always go out to Terre Haute, but our lead flow and sales had slowed, so we opened up a few different sources. For us we can take risks. For us it doesn't matter. We aren't driven by data straight into nightmares.

Here is a kind of nightmare I had: The app we use to show our appointments gives a picture of the front of the house, linked to Google maps, and I recognized my appointment instantly as the house I took Harvey to, and how it all worked out with Harvey was this: I dropped him at his family's house and he went inside, and then whatever happened happened, and no one has seen his brother ever since. There was a drop of Harvey's blood on the carpet in the master bedroom, and there was a square of carpet cut from the floor in the living room, but no one ever found anything beyond that.

Harvey stayed in custody a while and then was transferred to an assisted living facility where he lived for a few more months and then died in his sleep.

He sent me an email before he passed. I guess he got my address from an old website I had, and the email was in all caps and it said this:

COOK:

I'LL NEVER KNOW WHOSE GRAVE THAT WAS.
BUT GUESS WHAT, I KNOW WHO IT WILL BE FOR YOU.
IT'LL SAY HARVEY ON IT.
IT'LL SAY HARVEY FOREVER.

I didn't really know how to respond. I don't know if he was angry or happy. So, I just copied and pasted the email I'd received from Carlo Rovelli, about how he was too busy to respond, and I guess that was a good enough answer for him, because I never heard back.

The day after I got his message, my oldest daughter and I went to inspect the nameless grave, just to see if somehow Harvey had left us a kind of message—had gotten to the tombstone one last time before he was apprehended—but when we got there, nothing had changed.

It was winter but there wasn't snow on the ground, and my daughter and I blew our breath at each other, like we were blowing smoke.

"He's a little wrong," I said to my daughter. I looked at all the graves in the cemetery. "I don't just see Harvey on this grave. Every single grave here somehow says Harvey on it."

"Even better," my oldest daughter said. "You'll never feel bad if you have to steal anyone's flowers."

"Don't steal people's flowers," I told her.

"I won't," she said.

"Don't steal flowers, and don't eat in bed, and don't smoke weed, and don't do other people's homework, and don't roll your window down when it's twenty degrees, but feel free to. . ."

"I'm not folding her laundry."

"Fine," I said. "Then don't do those other things either."

Anyhow, I guess we'll see what Harvey's house is like underneath. It's always hard to tell from outside.

Hopefully it's a solid structure. The walls won't bow. The carpentry package won't be moldy. There'll be no standing, gray, shimmering water. No fortresses of cobwebs. No raccoon shit or raccoons in their little shredded newspaper nests, or snakes slithering in the Visqueen or snake skins shed in the folds.

Fingers crossed no wet hanging insulation that drags across the back of your neck as you move forth on hands and knees. Fingers crossed no fucking snakes.

My energy is good energy. I haven't been arrested since that last time.

So, here I go.
Feet first in the muck.
Catch that and paint it green, and wish me luck.

*The end
with wind*

Brian Allen Carr is an Aspen Words Finalist and a Wonderland Book Award winner. His short fiction has appeared in Granta, McSweeney's, Boulevard, and Pindeldyboz (IYKYK). His books include Opioid, Indiana, Motherfucking Sharks, and (coming soon) Bad Foundations.

ALSO BY CLASH BOOKS

EVERYTHING THE DARKNESS EATS
Eric LaRocca

EARTH ANGEL
Madeline Cash

I DIED TOO, BUT THEY HAVEN'T BURIED ME YET
Ross Jeffery

KILL THE RICH
Jack Allison & Kate Shapiro

I, CARAVAGGIO
Eugenio Volpe

PEST
Michael Cisco

THE LONGEST SUMMER
Alexandrine Ogundimu

ANYBODY HOME
Michael J. Seidlinger

DARRYL
Jackie Ess

GAG REFLEX
Elle Nash

HIGH SCHOOL ROMANCE
Marston Hefner

WE PUT THE LIT IN LITERARY
clashbooks.com

 @clashbooks @clashbooks /clashbooks

Email
clashmediabooks@gmail.com

Printed in the USA
CPSIA information can be obtained
at www.ICGtesting.com
JSHW081513040324
58548JS00007B/230

9 781955 904865